THIS IS HOW
I FIND HER

THIS IS HOW I FIND HER

SARA POLSKY

ALBERT WHITMAN & COMPANY
CHICAGO, ILLINOIS

Library of Congress Cataloging-in-Publication Data

Polsky, Sara.
This is how I find her / Sara Polsky.
pages cm
Summary: "High school junior Sophie has always had the burden of taking care of her
mother, who has bipolar disorder, but after her mother's hospitalization she must learn
to cope with estranged family and figure out her own life"— Provided by publisher.
ISBN 978-0-8075-7877-3 (hardback)
[1. Manic-depressive illness—Fiction. 2. Mental illness—Fiction. 3. Mothers and
daughters—Fiction. 4. Family problems—Fiction. 5. High schools—Fiction. 6.
Schools—Fiction.] I. Title.
PZ7.P7693Thi 2013
[Fic]—dc23
2013013317

10 9 8 7 6 5 4 3 2 1 LB 18 17 16 15 14 13

Cover design by Jenna Stempel.
Cover images ©iStockphoto.com/Shaun Lowe and Vladimir Piskunov.

For more information about Albert Whitman & Company
visit our website at www.albertwhitman.com

For my family.

ONE

ON THE FOURTH DAY OF JUNIOR YEAR, SOMETIME BETWEEN the second bell marking the start of chemistry class and the time I got home from school, my mother tried to kill herself.

———

This is how I find her:

I look for her when I come home, the way I always do, to say hello and tell her about my day. I head for her studio, which is what we call the little concrete-floored storage room in the basement of our building with our apartment number in marker on the plywood door. Our neighbors use their rooms for old chairs and crooked piles of boxes. Ours is almost empty except for my mother's easel in the center of the room and her paintings stacked against the walls. There's an ancient dresser next to the door, full of paints and colored pencils, paper clips and rubber bands and spare keys. The smell of paint hangs in the air and drifts under the plywood into the hallway.

The studio door is unlocked and I push it in without knocking, not wanting to interrupt my mother's work. A thin beam of light streams in from the window, not enough to paint by, and bright lamps in each corner cover the canvases in shadow and light. I expect to find my mother in her usual position, listening to classical music with the volume all the way up, right hand gripping her paintbrush, left hand moving as if she's conducting the violins and violas right through her stereo. She was there when I left for school this morning. She's been there every day and night for weeks, hardly sleeping, just painting.

My mother always paints when she's manic.

But not today. The studio is empty except for the half-done painting sitting on the easel, a blur of strong colors that looks to me like a woman running along a sunset beach. I can't tell whether the woman is fleeing or chasing.

Something about the painting feels off-balance to me, like a sentence stopped in the middle.

"Mom?" I ask, even though I can see she's not here.

I shut the studio door and head for the stairs in a walk that's almost a run. The painting looks abandoned in the empty, unlocked room.

My backpack thumps against my back, my shoes slap

unevenly against the steps, my breath huffs out, all in the rhythm of *hurry, hurry, hurry*. Some kids barrel into the stairwell on their way to play in what passes for a yard outside our building. I stumble into them and grab onto a higher step. One of the kids, a neighbor I babysit after school sometimes, calls out to me, but I don't answer. As soon as they're out of sight, I move even faster. *Hurry, hurry.* My leg muscles start to burn.

Finally, I get to the top floor, second-to-last door. I unlock it and rush into our apartment, my backpack still on. The place is chaotic. Since school started, I haven't had a chance to clean, and my mother never does. There's a trio of used coffee mugs on the table where we keep the mail, next to a teetering pile of envelopes and magazine subscription cards. My feet crinkle against shiny scraps of paper on the carpet. They're everywhere, as if a blizzard's worth of shredded catalogs snowed in our apartment while I was at school. I imagine my mother cutting them up, planning some kind of collage.

Where is she?

"Mom?" I ask the empty air of our apartment. Then I shout. "Mom!"

She doesn't answer. I move faster, toward the bedroom with her queen-sized bed in one corner and my twin bed in the other. My stomach swoops with nerves. Would I rather find her there or not know where she's gone? I'm not sure, and my feet keep moving forward without giving me a chance to think about it.

But when I get to the bedroom, my eyes get stuck on the numbers on the bedside clock. The clock face and I stare at each other, a contest I know I'll lose, for seconds that feel longer than they are. My eyes must know something the rest of me doesn't, because they won't let me look just those few inches farther to the left, toward my mother's bed. It's 3:34 p.m. The colon blinks at me: 3:34.

"Mom?" I say again.

There's still no answer, and when I force my eyes away from the clock, the first thing I see are her legs, dangling off the bed from the knees down, feet stopped just a few inches short of the floor as if resting themselves on the solid silence instead. I follow her legs upward to the rest of her, slanted across the bed, her head half on one pillow. Her eyes are closed, hair hanging ragged and long past the pale face I've noticed getting thinner again in the last few weeks. Her breath is so shallow I can't tell it's there at all until I put my ear right up against her mouth. Then some air tickles my cheek. I don't laugh.

When I look up, my hair drops off my shoulder and brushes against my mother's face. She doesn't stir.

There are the pills right in front of me. A few spill across her night table from a prescription bottle I don't recognize, its twisted-off childproof cap sitting nearby. And there's the glass. Just a regular kitchen glass with an inch of tap water at the bottom.

Terror crawls up through my stomach, stretches along my throat, and creeps into my mouth as I reach for the phone and press three numbers.

"My mom," I think I say, and "pills...half a bottle..."

Somehow, I get out enough complete thoughts to communicate the nature of my emergency. I confirm my address. Then I climb onto the bed, scrambling like a child much smaller than I am, and grab my mother's hand. I hold it until the sirens come.

TWO

"WOULD YOU LIKE US TO CALL SOMEONE FOR YOU?"

There's a nurse in mint-green scrubs standing in front of me, and I sit up so fast I bang my head on a poster. The frame rattles against the wall behind my head. Metal. I can't seem to take a deep enough breath, and my stomach turns over while I wait for the nurse to tell me how my mother is doing.

"Oof, that looked like it hurt," the nurse says instead. "Are you all right?"

Her words travel to me slowly, warped like I'm hearing her from the other side of a pane of glass. I blink. I'm in a hospital waiting room, on a tough vinyl chair with a hole in the seat. Before that I was in an ambulance, rocketing from my apartment to here. How did I get from that ambulance to this chair?

There are more important questions that crowd that one

out. Will my mother be okay? Where is she right now? Where did she get that bottle of pills?

Why didn't I know she had it?

"Your mother is going to be fine," the nurse says. I breathe more easily, in, out, in. The word settles into my stomach. *Fine*. Was she fine before?

The nurse looks at her clipboard to make sure she has my relationship to the patient right. I nod at her that she does. She tells me we've been lucky; my mother's just going to need to stay in the hospital for a little while.

Lucky.

It doesn't seem like the right word. Still, a few of the knots in my stomach unravel.

Then they come back when I think about how much it will cost for my mother to stay in the hospital.

And when I open my mouth and move my lips, no sound comes out.

"Would you like us to call someone for you?" the nurse asks again. "Your mother can't receive visitors yet, and you might be more comfortable at home. We can make a call if you need your dad or someone else to pick you up." Her words are efficient, routine, but her eyes are soft. Does she make this offer to everyone, or is she making an exception for me?

I shake my head. Then I finally get some words out.

"No, thank you." The words are froggy, like I've gone longer than just the past hour without speaking. She can't call my dad because I have no idea who he is. Someone else? I remember my mother reciting instructions to me; me, at eleven, nodding solemnly. *If anything ever happens to me, Sophie…*

I know where I have to go next. But I'd rather put off that phone call as long as possible.

I get up slowly, my jeans stuck to the backs of my legs. My bright blue backpack is still here, sitting on the chair next to me, and it makes me think of a puppy, loyally following me everywhere. My mother and I found it in a bin at a discount outlet store, and it has one badly sewn seam and someone else's initials—*JKP*—across the front. I sling it on, letting the weight of homework and textbooks settle onto my shoulders. I thank the nurse again and follow the exit signs out of the hospital. As I walk home, JKP's bag bounces against my back, keeping me company.

THREE

BY THE TIME I'M BACK ON THE TOP FLOOR OF OUR apartment complex, clicking the key into the lock, I've made a mental list of everything I need to do next. Wash the dirty coffee cups and take out the trash. Offer one of the neighbors any food from our fridge that might go bad. Tell the post office to hold our mail.

Pack two bags. One for my mother, one for me.

Clean up the pills on my mother's bedside table.

The first few chores are the same ones I do every day, and I start them mechanically, soaping the lime green sponge next to the sink and cleaning a plate, then letting the suds sit in last week's coffee mugs while I vacuum up the shredded catalog pieces from the front hall.

I'm so lost in my routine that I take a package of ground beef out of the fridge and unwrap it, preparing to make dinner. I do this—make dinner—every night. Every normal night. Now, as I stand in the empty kitchen with the light off, one hand holding a clump of ground beef, the memory of those nights drifts toward me through the dark.

———

My mother came into the kitchen when I was halfway through shaping the beef into patties, my hands goopy over the sink. She half danced, half walked into the room and dropped into a chair.

"Homework done?" she asked. I shrugged, but she didn't notice, already on her next thought. "Of course you've finished your homework already. Why do I even ask that anymore? It's always done."

I grinned at her over my shoulder. My mother assumed my work was done because I was a good student. I never told her it was because homework was the easiest part of my day, the only thing I could dash through without caring how it turned out.

I heard her hop up from the chair and start moving again, probably twirling around the table with her hair whipping out behind her. Even in her worn painting pants and baggy sweater, she moved like she was wearing floaty summer skirts.

"Good painting?" I asked without turning away from the

counter. I reached up to the cabinet for garlic powder and salt. I hesitated, looking over the rest of the spices, then grabbed the chili powder too.

"Hmm," my mother said. It was her usual answer, noncommittal, but I liked to think it meant she'd had a good day in her studio. I pictured her down there, arms flying, music playing, the old cushion on the floor in the corner where I would sit and draw while she worked.

Here, in the kitchen, she walk-danced closer to me. "What's for dinner, Sophie?" Her tone was teasing, like she knew what we were having but wanted to make me say it, like it was the setup for a joke.

"Burgers."

"Burgers, *again*?" She tried to sound fed up, but she couldn't quite keep the smile out of her voice.

"Yes, burgers *again*," I said. But I couldn't keep a straight face either. I dropped the patty I was holding and reached toward my mother. She skipped out of the way, laughing, before my goopy fingers could grab her. I laughed too. I put my elbow down on the counter so I wouldn't lose my balance. Then I waved the chili powder at her, to show they wouldn't be exactly the same burgers as usual. I flicked the cap open and started to sprinkle the spice on the patty in a swirly pattern.

My mother stopped in front of the fridge, which hummed

and thunked like it was part of our game. I covered a plate with a paper towel and set the burgers down. But before I could heat up the pan, my mother opened the freezer.

"Don't do that just yet," came her voice from behind the door. Ice-cold air wafted into the room. I turned to face my mother's voice and saw the bright orange streak across the white freezer. It began as a handprint and trailed off into a smear. My fault, an accident when we repainted the kitchen walls last year. I had started to wash it off right away, but my mother stopped me.

"It's like something you would have done when you were little, finger-painting with your friends," she'd said. "Let's keep it."

I'd wanted to ask *what friends?* I'd pictured Leila and James. Their tinier, rounder-cheeked kid faces, the way they were in our finger-painting days, not the way they looked now when I passed them in the halls at school, as they moved in groups of friends and I walked by myself. I'd winced, thinking of them. But I had stopped scraping the paint away.

My mother had told me it looked cheerful in the kitchen light, like a spark.

"Why shouldn't I finish the burgers?" I asked the part of my mother I could see below the freezer door. I was playing along; I already had a good idea why my mother didn't want me to cook dinner yet. I turned on the tap with my arm so I could wash the gunk off my hands.

"Close your eyes," she said. I did, and I heard something thud onto the counter, then the softer sounds of plastic containers landing next to it, then a few glassy ringing noises and metallic clanks.

"Now open."

I wasn't surprised by what I saw, but I gasped and dropped my jaw anyway, and my mother's laugh bubbled up from her stomach. She looked like she wanted to clap her hands, so delighted I giggled too. On the counter, two bowls, two spoons, a carton of ice cream and an ice cream scoop, sprinkles, and a squeeze-top bottle of chocolate sauce. The ice cream was cookie dough, our favorite flavor.

"Dessert first!" my mother said. She sent a bowl across the counter to me with one hand, like a Frisbee, and flipped the lid off the ice cream carton with the other. Still laughing, we dug in.

———

I blink and realize I'm standing in a dim kitchen with a fistful of ground beef. I'm squeezing it so tightly juice is dripping down into the sink. I look behind me out of habit, but of course my mother isn't here, and tonight I don't need to make dinner. Without the lights on in the kitchen, the orange paint on the freezer door is just a dull streak, ugly, not little kid cute. *What am I doing?*

13

I toss the beef in the garbage and think about the things still left on my list. Take out the trash.

Clean up the pills.

Pack the bags.

Go.

FOUR

THIS SCENE COULD BE A PHOTOGRAPH: ME, STANDING ON a porch, slightly off-center between two white wooden columns. My back is to the camera, long sleeves and jeans covering my tall, thin frame. My left hand is in front of me, reaching for the bell. The sleeve has fallen away to reveal the threaded bracelet on my wrist, made of leftover supplies from an art class my mother taught last year. My right arm stretches behind me, holding the pulled-up handle of a black wheely suitcase. The suitcase looks old, a few dusty footprints across the front, and on top of it is a duffel bag, not quite balanced. The last of the day's sun slants onto the bright green lawn behind me. The photo could be called *Arrival*. Or maybe *Visitor*.

Then I hear my mother's voice in my mind. *It needs more shadow, Sophie.* Suddenly it's a painting, not a photo, and she's reaching in to dab some gray and black here and there, edging the columns, deepening the sky. Now there are a million hidden layers to the scene.

Thinking about it, about my mother, I flinch—and that's when the door opens.

My cousin Leila stands there in the outfit I recognize from school—lavender tank top, gray sweater, dark gray skirt, high black boots. Eye makeup, even though it's just a Tuesday evening. I guess maybe she's on the way out to practice with her band.

We're the same height and have the same shade of dark brown hair, but mine hangs wearily down my back, split at the ends, while hers bounces along her shoulders. After the startled moment when she opens the door and finds me there, we avoid each other's eyes.

We're good at that. We've been doing it for years.

Leila opens the door wider and steps back, holding onto the knob as I twist my suitcase through the door.

"Sophie, I'm—" she says, as I finish wrestling the bag inside and start to pull it along the hardwood floor. The squeaking of the wheels drowns out Leila's voice. She's *what? Sorry? Glad to see me?* Knowing her, neither expression seems likely. I don't prompt her for the rest of her sentence.

Leila is still looking at the floor when Aunt Cynthia

hurries down the stairs, her feet coming into view first, then her neatly pressed pants and sweater set and pinned-back hair. I know she wears fancier suits to work, but she still looks like she could be on her way to an office.

She passes Leila in the hall as if she knows exactly where she's going, but when she sees me, she stops instantly. We look at each other.

One of Aunt Cynthia's arms moves toward me, and I wonder if she's going to give me a hug. I stiffen, not meaning to, and the arm drops. I think of the conversation we had a few hours ago, when I called her cell phone to explain that my mother would be staying at the hospital at least overnight.

"If you don't mind…I mean, my mother always said that if anything happened to her, I should come stay with you until she's better," I rambled into the phone, shifting from one foot to the other in my kitchen, wondering if I should have taken the nurse up on her offer to call someone for me instead. Wishing there were another someone I could have called. Wishing I hadn't promised my mother I would do this. I knew I could manage in our apartment alone for a few days.

Aunt Cynthia's voice finally drifted back to me just when I was about to say *Hello? Is anybody there?*

"Oh. Yes, you can stay here." She sounded distracted, frazzled, her voice shaky at first. Then, suddenly brisker, she started firing questions at me about my mother. "Did they have her on lithium? Are they switching her to something else? What about vitamins and a sleeping pill?"

"She was on lithium, yes," I said, practically spitting out the "yes." I glared at the wall, trying to put into my voice just how much I didn't want to answer Aunt Cynthia's questions. How little I thought she deserved answers after five years of not asking.

She didn't ask anything else.

Now, in her front hallway, Aunt Cynthia tells me to come in, even though I clearly already did.

She reaches out for one of my bags. I don't move toward her, but I also don't stop her when she takes the duffel from my hand. My whole body is braced for her to say…something.

It's your fault, Sophie.

You weren't careful enough.

Didn't you see the warning signs? I would have. I would have stopped her.

"John?" she calls instead.

I hear quick steps from another room, and then Cynthia's husband joins us in the now-crowded space between the front door and the stairs. Uncle John has on a button-down shirt and a tie with tiny dots, the kinds of clothes he wears to his job as an architect. I realize I have no idea what time it is.

Did Uncle John and Aunt Cynthia come home early because of me? Or did I spend so long at the hospital that it isn't even early anymore?

We all stand there for a minute, staring at the empty air between us. No one says anything about why I'm there. No one says anything at all.

Then Uncle John clears his throat. He's taller than the rest of us and wire thin, and I have to look up to meet his eyes.

"Sophie," Uncle John says. "Welcome."

He takes the duffel from Aunt Cynthia and reaches over to grab my suitcase with his other hand. When he punches the handle down, the plastic clicking sound echoes in the quiet. "Come, you're in the guest room upstairs."

Before I follow him, I look back toward the front door, to where Leila was standing just a minute ago. But the door is already closed. The photo-perfect lawn is out of sight, and Leila is gone.

FIVE

UNCLE JOHN DEPOSITS MY BAGS IN THE CENTER OF THE guest room, which is a creamy beige-white everywhere except for the two dark dots the bags make on the carpet. We study them for a few seconds in silence, as if they have secrets to tell us.

"There are leftovers from dinner in the kitchen if you're hungry," Uncle John says. "Just pasta and sauce." He takes a step back toward the door. "We'll leave you to get settled in. Your aunt cleared out the closet, so it's all yours."

Then he leaves, and I sit down hard on the bed, the words *your aunt* bouncing around in my brain. Even though I know her as Aunt Cynthia, I haven't actually thought of her as *my aunt* in a long time. And this isn't my closet or my room.

Aunt Cynthia's house is quieter than our apartment, where we could always hear another family arguing down the hall or kids shouting and stomping their way up and down the stairs. Here, the only sound I notice is the soft ticking of the clock. I look at it and think of the clock by my mother's bed, flashing at me, 3:34, 3:34, 3:34.

This has always been my mother's room.

Aunt Cynthia and Uncle John called it the guest room then too, when we would sometimes stay here for two or three weeks at a time, but I was sure we were the only guests they ever had. Whenever we showed up—in the middle of the night or right after school or on Saturday morning before breakfast—the room was empty. Aunt Cynthia always took my mother's arm and led her gently up the stairs, to the right, into this room. My mother curled up on the bed and mumbled something about how tired and scared she was, the words melting together as her head hit the pillow.

"I know, Amy, I know," Aunt Cynthia would say, tugging the covers from underneath my mother and pulling them over her instead.

Aunt Cynthia smoothed down my mother's hair the same way she patted Leila's sometimes before bed, and it made me imagine my mother small, the way Leila and I were. When she left my mother there to sleep, she shut the door softly behind her and shooed Leila and me away from where we waited outside, telling us my mother needed her rest. Sometimes I caught Aunt Cynthia on the phone later, saying things about appointments and medications to someone on the other end. She looked just as tired as my mother did, her short hair frizzy and wild around her head instead of neat and pinned the way it was when she went to work.

For however long my mother and I stayed with Aunt Cynthia, this small, pale guest room was one of the few places in the house that was off-limits to Leila and me. Aunt Cynthia kept us entertained elsewhere. She wouldn't let us sponge paint her walls the way my mother sometimes did, but she taught us card games and gave us old toys she brought down from the attic. They used to belong to her and my mother, and somehow Aunt Cynthia had a new one every time we came to stay, a surprise for Leila and me. A distraction.

When Aunt Cynthia wasn't watching, Leila and I still sneaked upstairs and hovered outside the guest room door. We'd wiggle our fingers at each other and tug on our ears, daring each other in our own secret language to reach out and open the door. But it was mostly a game, both of us giggling whenever our fingertips brushed the doorknob. We never made it inside, never managed to get a peek at what my mother was up to.

——————

And now I'm the one in here, door closed, blank walls all around me. It's the first time I've ever had my own room.

I get up from the bed and start moving around quietly, even though I don't need to worry about waking up my mother the way I do at home. I don't unpack. Instead, I pull open the drawers in the dresser and desk and run my fingers around the crinkly paper liners inside. They have a pattern of pastel flowers, cheery and at odds with the fog that always seemed to hang over this room when my mother stayed in it.

I open the empty closet and peer at its back wall. I'm not sure what I'm looking for. Maybe a sign that my mother really was here, some folded note or scratched-in message or doodle she might have left me. Something telling me what she was doing in here, all those times. Something telling me why.

But by the time I'm done searching, it's completely dark outside, and I've found nothing at all.

SIX

I WAKE UP TO A THUMPING NOISE ON MY LEFT, THE SOUND of someone going up or down the stairs. I don't remember going to bed, but I'm lying in it now, looking up at the ceiling, the steady soft noise of the clock in my ear. I turn toward it.

It's 7:00, so the feet on the stairs could be anyone's. Leila racing for breakfast before school; Aunt Cynthia or Uncle John rushing out the door to work. I decide it's Leila, stomping up or down in her loud boots. She's the one most likely to be running late. She's never been a morning person.

But I am. This is the latest I've slept in as long as I can remember. And now that I'm awake, something about the room still feels strange, like some essential ingredient is missing. Then I remember what: my mother.

I don't think anyone is going to come looking for me, so

I let myself lie there, staring up at the ceiling. I conjure up the memory of my usual morning, holding it around me like a blanket.

"Soph?" If this were our apartment, that would be my mother's voice from across the room, a not-really-trying-to-keep-quiet whisper. She's an early bird too, most of the time. "You awake?"

"Of course," I say. "I have school. It's Wednesday."

My mother makes a *pfft* sound. "You have hours yet. Come on. To the kitchen!" She swings her legs out of bed and slowly stands up, pretending that her joints are aching. Then she dashes across the room and grabs my arm to pull me out of bed. "Up, up, up!"

I can't help the laugh that slips out as she tugs on my arm and I stumble out of bed. When I get to the kitchen, she's already pulled ingredients out of the fridge: eggs for omelets, chocolate syrup for homemade waffles and ice cream. We spend the hours until I have to leave for school whipping up breakfast and eating it together.

———

But now, all I'm doing is staring up at Aunt Cynthia's guest room ceiling, tracing the bumps and grains of the plaster under the white paint. Instead of seeing the elaborate breakfasts on the blank screen above me, other images start to play there instead. Our messy apartment. My mother's

25

painting of the running woman. My sneakers on the stairs, dodging the kids on their way down. The white mystery pills, spilled across the table by the bed. The glass of water, nearly empty.

I sit up.

I swing my legs out from under the covers, slowly, one after the other, like my mother when she's planning to catch me off guard by dashing across the room. I'm still wearing the jeans and long-sleeved shirt I had on yesterday. The same outfit that came home from school and went down to the studio, then up to the apartment. That walked across the shredded catalog pages and into the bedroom. The outfit that found my mother lying across her bed, diagonal and still.

I take it off. The rest of my clothes are still rolled up inside the wheely suitcase on the floor, shirts and pants spiraled to fit as much as possible into the small bag, toothbrush holder and hairbrush and balled pairs of socks stuffed into any leftover space. I grab a T-shirt at random and get dressed.

———

Downstairs, Aunt Cynthia's eyebrows lift when she sees me. Her mouth falls slightly open. She stops halfway between the coffeemaker and the counter, coffeepot held aloft in one hand.

"I didn't think we'd see you today," she says, starting to move again, toward the two tall aluminum mugs waiting next to the sink. I listen to the coffee stream into the cups, then I sniff in the smell. Hazelnut.

There's a lilt of surprise in Aunt Cynthia's voice, and I know I was right; no one would have come upstairs to get me up.

Then I register Aunt Cynthia's words, *I didn't think we'd see you today*. Something about those words, the light way she says them, penetrates the thick cloud over my brain. I realize that since I got here, she still hasn't called me by my name or said a word about my mother. She hasn't told me whether she thinks what happened is my fault.

Just say it! I think at her, and I don't even know what I'm expecting to hear. But Aunt Cynthia keeps moving through her morning routine, snapping lids onto the coffee cups and leaving the pot to soak in the sink. She points out the bread drawer, exactly where it was when I was eleven, and the cold cuts in the fridge for sandwiches. Those are the same too—turkey, ham, salami—and it's strange to me that everything around me feels so familiar when the circumstances are so different. Aunt Cynthia tells me, still in that same light voice, that I can ride with Leila to school if I'm going.

She can't hear me yelling at her from inside my head.

She doesn't realize I'm actually waiting for a different

voice, to tell me she's making waffles with ice cream for breakfast, to send me off on my walk to school with a *see you later* and a wink, maybe to hint that there's a note hidden somewhere in my backpack.

And I just twist my fingers together and stand there, saying nothing.

Ten minutes later, I'm in the front seat of Leila's car, my backpack braced between my legs and the dashboard. I haven't eaten breakfast. One corner of my math book is digging into my right knee, but I don't want to ask my cousin if I can move the seat back. I'd rather we both just pretend I'm not actually in the car.

Leila jitters next to me. She jiggles her left leg, sips from her coffee, drums her fingers against the steering wheel, hums a few bars of music, over and over again.

Usually, as I walk to school in the morning, Leila drives fast past me, windows open, elbow out, music blaring so loudly it seems to echo down the street long after she's gone by. But this morning, with me in the car, she keeps the music off and inches carefully out of the driveway. Her car is silver and still looks new, nothing like the ancient, battered two-door my mother and I share, sitting unused in the parking lot at our apartment complex.

As Leila backs into the street, turns left at the corner and then right at the next, the silence crackles around us like radio static.

Then Leila's voice breaks through. "How's your mom?" she asks. She says *your mom* and not *Aunt Amy*, as if she doesn't actually know her.

"I don't really know yet," I say. I shift, trying to get comfortable, but the math book just pushes more sharply into my leg. "They told me she's going to be fine. But she was getting her stomach pumped yesterday, so I couldn't see her." I say it as matter-of-factly as I can. Then I think of Aunt Cynthia, who might be on the way to some kind of record for how long she can go without mentioning my mother. I wonder how she would react if I said it to her, just like that. *Your sister got her stomach pumped yesterday.*

"Oh," is all Leila says. We slide to a stop at a light behind a long line of cars, and I wait for her to say more. Maybe a question about what the doctors will do for my mother next or about when she'll be allowed to have visitors.

But she doesn't say anything. That one *oh* just hangs there. I open my mouth, but all that comes out is air. I can't think of anything to say other than *what's your problem?* so I hold myself back. Do Leila and Aunt Cynthia really not have a million questions about my mother, about what happened and how she's doing? I feel the questions hovering in the air around me.

After a minute, Leila reaches forward and flicks the radio on. The music balloons into the space and Leila starts humming again, shoving everything else—my mother, that lingering *oh*—out of the way.

It feels like the music is pushing me out of the way too.

I scrunch myself down, closer to the door, and try to remember a time when car rides with Leila were fun.

"How fast do you think we can go?"

My mother's question floated back to us from the front seat. She always had something like that, some kind of unanswerable question or game for us. She shouted over the radio, and her words blurred together as if she had hit the fast-forward button on her own voice. *Howfastdoyouthinkwecango?* Our car was headed down an empty stretch of road outside of town, windows down so the air could breeze across the seats. We always kept the car windows cracked open in the summer, because even the thin stream of August heat from outside was better than the way the air conditioner rattled and clanked. My mother had a country music station on—the car was the only place she listened to music that wasn't classical—and we caught snatches of her singing along, hitting words like *love* and *dog* and *cry*. She was singing loudly, sometimes making up her own lyrics and always out of tune with the voice on the radio. Whenever she hit a note particularly wrong, Leila and I would snort and shush each other, trying not to laugh too loudly.

We looked up when my mother turned to us. We'd stretched the skirts of our new sundresses across our knees to make flat surfaces for our dolls to play, and we were focused on their adventure, a trip to New York City. I tugged at my skirt, knowing Aunt Cynthia, who had given us the dresses on the last day of school in June, wouldn't be happy about how we were stretching them out.

"It's a new school present," Aunt Cynthia had said when she handed us the bags. "You're officially middle schoolers now." Coming up behind us, Uncle John had groaned and chimed in, "And about to become ten times more obnoxious because of it." But he ruffled Leila's hair and grinned at me, and we were pretty sure he was joking.

In the front seat, my mother turned away from the road to face us. "What do you think?" she asked again. Her long hair fluttered in the breeze from the windows, as if an invisible hand was lifting up strands and laying them back down against her shoulders. "How fast?"

I giggled. Leila set down the doll she was holding on the seat between us and leaned forward, focusing totally on my mother. We liked the summers because my mother watched us, and she was always okay with breaking the rules. We liked it when she talked fast but we could understand her anyway, as if her words were a code meant just for us.

My mother was still looking at us and us at her, the road whizzing by outside the windows without any of us watching it. Somehow, my mother still kept steering the wheel through the road's twists and turns. As if the car were telling her which way to go. Or she'd driven it this way before.

"Well, are you ready?" she asked. We nodded solemnly, our dolls forgotten, completely replaced by our game with my mother. She turned back to the road. "Let's see how fast."

———

A noise that sounds like *grr-hem* snaps my attention back to where I am now, aware of the car, the radio tuned to Leila's favorite station, that sharp corner of my math book.

I twist uncomfortably in my seat, wishing I could go back to that moment, full of anticipation for what my mother would do next.

Leila is looking at me, and I realize the sound must have been her clearing her throat. Did she say something? I wait a second to see if she'll repeat it.

But she doesn't. I look past her, out the driver's side window, and see that we're already stopped in the school parking lot. Leila always parks in the small overflow lot at the back, the one that's an entire school building away from the windows of the principal's office. The radio's still on, but Leila's hand is on the key in the ignition, ready to turn the car off.

A clump of people is walking toward us, each person trying to fit on the narrow mulch median bordered with stones that separates the rows of the lot. I recognize a few of them as friends of Leila's from the jazz band she sings in, but I know only one: James, a tall boy with dark hair who seems to flop as he moves, as if all his limbs are noodles.

Or I did know him. A shorter, younger version of him who used to play foursquare on the blacktop outside our elementary school with Leila and me, who would walk home with us almost every afternoon so we could run around in Leila's backyard or ride bikes through her neighborhood. Aunt Cynthia worked with James's mom, and he would stay with us until one of his parents came to pick him up for dinner.

He used to be my friend too. Maybe even more my friend than Leila's.

In my head, I hear the rubber playground ball thwack against the pavement as James bounces it to our side of the chalk square. I hear Leila shout his name, annoyed, as the bounce goes high and she misses.

She turns to me, her expression telling me she expects me to get the ball, but I shake my head. "No way," I tell her. "It was in your corner."

33

James grins at me as Leila goes running after the ball, a grin that says *hey, isn't it nice to make* her *do the chasing sometimes?* He produces a melting candy bar from his pocket and offers me half. I smile back from my quadrant, chocolate dripping from my fingers, and we're allies.

But I don't know if he remembers any of that. As he and the girl next to him look toward where we're parked, I turn away from the window, not wanting to make eye contact.

Here, in the car, Leila is still looking at me, her expression asking, *are you going to move, or what?*

I guess she decides the answer is *or what*, because she huffs, turns the car off, and shakes her head a little as she opens her door. She swings one leg out, then the other, then reaches around her seat for her bag. She gives me one more glance over her shoulder.

Something about that look finally triggers me and I move, working my backpack out from under the glove compartment. My eyes skim over the initials on the front for the thousandth time, and I wonder who JKP is and whether I could slip into her life as easily as I slide her bag onto my back. I wish.

Leila and I step out of our opposite sides of the car at the same time, shutting the doors with thuds that are almost synchronized. But that's where the symmetry ends. She hits the door lock button and jumps right into a conversation with her friends. I hunch over, hook my thumbs under my backpack straps, and start to walk away.

I glance back once to see James passing Leila one of his headphones so she can hear the song he's listening to. She leans in and starts to tap her foot. They've always had that in common, music, the way my mother and I have art.

I'm facing the school again, walking, when I hear one of Leila's friends, a girl whose voice I don't recognize. "Hey," she says, "who was that?"

"What?" Leila asks, and it's *what are you talking about, not what did you say.*

"The girl in the car with you," her friend says. "Who was that?"

"Oh," Leila says. In the next second of silence, I imagine her waving one arm carelessly to say *Her? She's nobody.*

Then she says, "That's my cousin, Sophie."

James says nothing, and I don't wait to hear if the girl I don't know will say anything else. Instead I walk faster, listening only to the *slap-slap* of my sneakers on the pavement and the jingle of the zippers on my backpack. The more quickly I get inside, the sooner I can lose myself, just one in the stream of eight hundred other students heading for class, hurrying to beat the bell.

SEVEN

BUT HIDING IS HARDER THAN I THOUGHT.

In math class, we're working quietly through a set of equations Mr. Borakov has scrawled across the dry erase board, our daily warm-up, when the phone in the corner buzzes. It's a loud staccato sound that makes at least half the class jump and look toward the yellowed cradle on the wall. I put my head down, focusing on the next trig problem. *Please don't be for me.*

I punch some more numbers into my calculator, trying to get the equation to graph correctly. In front of me, there are at least two people using their calculators to play games while Mr. Borakov is on the other side of the room. I could play too; all the school graphing calculators have the same games saved by bored students from some other year. But I don't look for them. Math is one of the few classes I actually like. The numbers and symbols are a language I don't completely understand, but I believe I can if I keep trying. Eventually, the equations will form complete sentences. *X* plus *Y* will equal something: an answer, concrete and unambiguous.

Mr. Borakov says a few words into the phone and sets it down with a click, and everyone looks up again. "Sophie Canon?" he calls. It's only the fifth day of school, so his glance skims over the entire class, not completely sure which student I am.

In the second seat in the third row from the right, I nod and put my hand up, just slightly, to the level of my shoulder. Mr. Borakov's gaze finds me and stops.

"Your guidance counselor needs to see you," he says. "Just give me what you've done so far so you can get credit for today."

I'm only half aware of tearing the page from my notebook and putting my backpack on, of passing the sheet of paper to Mr. Borakov and hearing his thanks as I leave the room. I don't know if anyone in the class is watching or wondering why I'm leaving. There's only one thought in my head. *What's wrong now?*

––––––

My guidance counselor is still in a meeting when I get to her office, so the secretary tells me to have a seat in one of the chairs lined up between her desk and the door. "Her meeting's running a bit late. Or maybe you just walked here a lot faster than everyone else does," the secretary says. Her voice is dry when she adds, "I have no idea why people aren't more excited to get a call from the guidance office."

I try to laugh, but I can hear how fake it sounds. So I just shrug at her. I have no idea how fast I got here. I was too busy wondering what my guidance counselor needed to tell me. Is my mother worse than the nurse said she'd be? Was Aunt Cynthia or the hospital trying to reach me at school?

I sit. The guidance office chairs are all fabric and cushion, nothing like the plastic-y hospital chair I spent hours in yesterday afternoon. But the feeling I have sitting in it is the same, the braids of anxiety twisting themselves together again in my stomach. I jiggle my legs. That makes me think of how jittery Leila was in the car this morning, then of seeing James and Leila sharing headphones in the parking lot, then of the way Leila shrugged me off. I stop moving and wait.

"Sophie, hi!" My guidance counselor comes around the corner in her usual neat dark suit and pumps, hands out in greeting. She's smiling and says my name with an exclamation point, and I must look confused, because when she stops in front of me, her eyebrows V downward. "Sophie?"

"Hi, Ms. Wilkins," I say. *Why is she acting so cheerful about this?* I follow her into her office, where she waves me into another cushy chair.

She sits too and riffles through a mess of papers on her desk until she pulls out a single white sheet. Through the back of it, I see heavy black lines, what looks like a chart.

"Here's your new schedule," Ms. Wilkins says, handing it over.

New schedule?

Ms. Wilkins is still talking. "You've lost your study hall and we had to switch you to a different period of English because there wasn't an art class at your level in your free period, but it's a pretty minor change." She points to the afternoon time slots on my printout.

My eyes follow her finger down the page, but I'm not really looking or listening. Now I remember that I came to see Ms. Wilkins on the first day of school, just last week, because I'd been put in study hall instead of art by accident.

The only thing I wanted that day was to be back at my black-topped table in the art room, sitting quietly in the same alphabetical order as always, closing my eyes and trying to make the shapes I saw behind my eyelids.

If my mother ever asked me if I had a good painting day, I wanted to be able to say *hmm* too, in that same satisfied humming voice. To share a secret smile with her that said *I know what that's like.*

Ms. Wilkins must have called me in here just to tell me that she straightened out the schedule glitch. Not to talk about anything else.

Not to tell me that something else happened to my mother.

"Sophie?"

I look up. Ms. Wilkins looks like she's expecting me to answer a question, but I didn't hear it. I wait, the way I did with Leila in the car this morning, for Ms. Wilkins to repeat herself.

"Does that work for you? The new schedule?"

I nod. I shift forward in my chair, ready to get up.

"Good," Ms. Wilkins says. "We'll have to make another appointment soon to start planning for college applications, okay? Your math and science grades are strong, and your work in art, of course. You may want to start talking to Ms. Triste about what kinds of things to work on this year so you have art samples ready to go."

"College," I say dully. "Sure."

Ms. Wilkins reshuffles another pile of papers, then runs her thumb down the side of the stack. The papers make a *zzzwip* noise. "How's everything else going so far? Year off to a good start?"

I freeze.

In the next few seconds of silence, while I'm superglued to the edge of my chair, I try out a few phrases in my head.

Not really. My mother's in the hospital. Actually, I thought that's why you called me in here. She overdosed on pills. I didn't even know she had them.

I need to change the address you have on file because I'm living with my aunt and uncle right now. It should only be for a little while.

Ms. Wilkins waits, her eyes moving from the papers up to my face. She doesn't know anything about my mother.

I could tell her now.

But all those sentences are locked away in my brain, separated by a thick wall from the regular words I let myself use every day. There's a door in the wall, but it has a heavy padlock and rusted-over hinges. I don't have the key.

And when I open my mouth, somehow my feet move instead, propelling me up from the chair. Standing by the door of Ms. Wilkins's office, the only words that come out are a lie.

"Yeah," I tell her, trying and failing to smile. "So far the year's going fine."

———

I eat lunch where I always do: sitting in the hallway by myself, back against my locker, textbook balanced across my knees. I chew a bite of my turkey sandwich for as long as it takes to read a word problem in my math book. Then I swallow, click more lead out of my pencil, and start writing an equation.

41

The words become simpler numbers and symbols and I do problem after problem until my homework is finished. It's the first time all day that I feel focused. Grounded.

The bell hasn't rung yet, so I reach into my bag for my history book. When I pull it out, there's an envelope stuck between the book and its brown paper bag cover, the name of the electric company printed in the upper left corner. But there's no bill inside. Just words scrawled across the back in my mother's handwriting.

> *Dear JKP,*
>
> *Today you're a famous ballet dancer in school for a few weeks between tours with your company. You've got a big part in The Nutcracker for the holidays, so you're gliding through the hallways, and none of your teachers dare ask whether you finished the homework. (Of course, being you, you did.)*
>
> *Have a great day!*
>
> *Love,*
>
> *Mom*

This is another one of my mother's games: imagining who JKP could be and leaving notes for each of her many identities—debutante, guitarist, dancer, art thief—scrawled on scrap paper in my backpack. Sets of instructions for me on how to be a different person.

I stare at the note, the letters getting blurrier below me,

until there are feet thundering past me through the hall and the lockers above me start to open and slam shut again. Lunch is over.

The voice in the back of my head starts whispering then, as I toss out the last bit of my sandwich and put away my history book. It whispers all the way through chemistry and gym, as I balance equations and count push-ups and do two laps around the track with the rest of the class. It keeps asking if this was the moment yesterday that my mother poured herself the glass of water and opened the bottle of pills. *Did it happen now?* The voice has a question for me between each jumping jack. *How about now?* I count crunches under my breath. *Yesterday, while I was doing just this sit-up, was that when she swallowed the first one?*

The bell for seventh period interrupts the endless whispered questions, and I take out the schedule Ms. Wilkins gave me and walk toward *English, Mr. Jackson, Room 210.* Around me in the hallway, people are saying hello and shouting plans for after school. I keep my head down and watch my feet step on the lines between the floor tiles. Line, square, line, square, line.

When I open the door to 210, the first person whose eyes I meet is Leila. The second is James.

I stop three steps into the classroom, stuck in place just like I was in the guidance office.

Someone bumps into my backpack from behind and I trip forward. "Excuse me," a loud girl's voice says.

The teacher looks up at that, and I finally move away from the door and hold my new schedule out in his direction. I'm gripping the paper so hard I feel it crumpling in my hand, leaving a dent at the top. I refuse to look toward the desk where Leila sits.

"My guidance counselor reassigned me to this class," I say. *And I wish she could switch me right back out of it.*

"Right," Mr. Jackson says. "I think I got an email about that." He squints at his computer monitor, clicking the mouse a few times, and I wait. The ceiling's buzzing fluorescent lights reflect off the frames of his glasses and the shiny top of his head. The second bell rings. Students shuffle in and take their seats in the U-shaped row of desks until I'm the only one still standing.

"I can't find it," Mr. Jackson says, straightening up and turning to face me. He peers at my schedule. "Sorry about that. What's your name again?"

I feel the rest of the class sitting there, waiting for this to be over. Out of the corner of my eye, I see James watching me. And I think I see the edge of Leila's mouth turn up in a smirk. I remember again how I imagined her this morning, waving one arm after me in a gesture that said, *Her? She's nobody.*

"Sophie Canon," I say. But somehow my voice runs out halfway through, so I swallow the "on." My face starts to feel hot.

"Well, welcome," Mr. Jackson says. He sweeps one hand toward an empty desk at the back of the U. "Have a seat."

He launches into an explanation of this week's reading assignment, interrupting himself to remind everyone that words from the first few chapters will be on Friday's vocab quiz, but I catch only about one word in every six he says. When I glance at the other side of the room, I think I see James looking toward me, but his eyes flick away quickly, and I'm not actually sure he was looking at all.

I doodle absently in the corner of the vocabulary worksheet someone passes me, sketching towers of connected triangles and cubes. Mr. Jackson's words fade into the background and the other voice, the whispery one, comes back. *Was it now?* I look over at the clock and imagine the ticking I'm too far away to hear. I try to draw another cube, but my hand is shaking and it comes out crooked. *Or now?*

Then the voice starts asking another question. *What if?* What if my mother hadn't been breathing when I leaned over her yesterday? What if I hadn't come home right after school and run upstairs to look for her? What if she had taken the pills somewhere other than our apartment?

Panic rises up through my body as my imagination keeps

45

asking questions, wilder and more far-fetched, taking me far away from class and my desk and the vocabulary book sitting on it.

And I wonder: if I'm listening to a voice in my head, a voice that makes me scared, does that mean I'm crazy too?

EIGHT

I DON'T GO TO ART.

By the time English ends, the questions have grown to a crescendo in my head, too loud for me to hear anything Mr. Jackson says. The bell pulls me out of my thoughts just as I'm starting to imagine my mother's funeral, everyone in black dresses and suits except for my mother's artist friends in long sweaters and scarves. Finding myself in my seat again feels like waking up from a nightmare. I'm shaking and terrified.

I need to see my mother.

I need to reassure myself that what I remember is what happened; that what I'm imagining isn't real. That I found her and called the ambulance; that she's at the hospital and on her way to being okay.

When the bell rings, I'm one of the first out of the

classroom, backpack on, feet almost skidding across the hard hallway tiles. I turn right and hurry down the stairs, thinking only of yesterday afternoon, when I climbed up to our apartment so quickly I felt it in the backs of my legs. I try to breathe evenly, to keep my heart from racing. My mother is the one who is anxious, who can sometimes talk and move impossibly quickly. I am calm.

I'm calm.

The nearest exit is past the art room, where I'm supposed to be spending the next period. As I walk that way, people weave around me and peel off into classrooms; as I get closer to the art room, I recognize a few of my old classmates ahead of me.

The hallways suddenly empty out with only a minute to go before the late bell. I stop across from the art room, diagonal to the window in the wooden door, and look inside. Ms. Triste stands at the board, back to the door, all in black with her short curls bobbing around her head. Next to her is one of her paintings, a canvas taller than she is with red and blue squares fading into each other, soft and mesmerizing.

Something crosses my vision—a dark stripe that doesn't belong in Ms. Triste's painting. I refocus my eyes and the stripe is a person, one of my classmates, Natalie Greenberg. She's shorter than me, so I can see where the blue streak in her hair begins at her scalp. We've been in the same art class for two years, but we've barely ever spoken.

The late bell rings.

"Are you coming in?" a voice asks, and I realize Natalie is talking to me. She has one hand on the half-open door, one of her feet in its combat boot already in the classroom.

I shake my head at the same moment that a voice calls down the hall, "Hey, Sophie!"

I turn my head just as James skids to a stop on the tile floor next to me, his hair still flopping.

I look down at the floor, then look up again when I hear a soft click. Natalie has disappeared into Ms. Triste's classroom. From the other side of the door, she glances quickly back at where James and I are standing, but I can't read her expression at all. Is she going to tell Ms. Triste I'm out here?

"Hey," James says, looking curiously at the door and then at me. "Where are you heading?"

His real voice is deeper than the little-kid voice he's had in my head all this time. When he says *hey*, it's like I can feel his words rumbling up from my chest.

I take a deep breath. Then I shrug.

"Nowhere," I tell him.

I can almost see the words *yeah, right* cross his face. But he doesn't say them.

A memory hits me suddenly, socking me in the gut from

out of nowhere. Leila and James and I are eight, playing in Leila's backyard after school. When we set off into the woods behind her house for hide-and-seek, James follows me, even when I remind him we're supposed to be hiding. He reaches out and grabs my hand, his sticky from the candy he's always eating, and I start to blush, imagining Leila teasing us. But I don't actually mind and I don't let go. I follow him farther into the woods, to a pair of barbed wire fences standing there between the trees, guarding nothing. They're covered over with vines, like a tunnel, and when I follow James inside, I know Leila won't be able to find us here. When she comes looking, maybe we'll jump out and surprise her. We sit in the shade from the vines, splitting a stack of Oreos and playing tic-tac-toe on a grubby napkin.

It feels like a very long time ago.

"You rushed out of English like something was wrong," James says now. "And Leila said you were staying with her, and I was coming down this hallway and saw you, so I wondered…"

You wondered what?

I wonder if Leila told him anything else about why I'm staying at her house. But I can't tell from looking at him exactly what he knows. He's always been like that, quiet and slightly hard to read. When we were younger, I liked that I was one of the few people he talked to. But now one of Mr.

Jackson's vocabulary words, one of the few things I heard last period before the voice took over my brain, pops into my head: inscrutable.

I think of the sentences I tried out in my head when Ms. Wilkins asked me about my year so far. *My mother is in the hospital for a little while, so I'm staying with Leila and her parents.* I think about saying that to James, telling him I'm on my way to see my mother now. Telling him there's a voice in my head reminding me about the way I found her yesterday, lying still across her bed. Wondering what would have happened if I hadn't found her.

But there's still that rusty door in my mind, with its heavy padlock and no key. All of the words I'm thinking are hidden behind it. Just imagining what I could say, my stomach starts to cramp nervously. And I can't picture how James would react. Would he ask questions? Or would he look as if he'd always suspected, from his glimpses of my mother when we were kids, that something about her wasn't quite normal?

So instead I just ask, "Don't you have a class?"

He shrugs. "Band, but they're working with winds for the first half of the period."

Band. In fourth grade, we were allowed to choose instruments for band and orchestra. I played violin for two years until they let me quit. Leila only ever wanted to audition for chorus. And James picked drums. Before the teacher called his name to start drumming at the tryouts, he just sat quietly on the stool behind the set, looking down from beneath his hair the way he always did. He and I were usually as quiet and calm as Leila was loud, until we were by ourselves— then we could start talking or playing a game and be as noisy as she was. But when the band director gave James the cue, he threw himself into the rhythms and became the louder, fiercer version of himself, right in front of everybody. Now, I wonder if the people who play in the school band with him think he's like that all the time.

Maybe these days he is like that all the time.

For a second, I see it: James as the mysterious, inscrutable rocker dude with dark hair that swings around as he bangs his head while drumming. For some reason, the thought makes my cheeks feel warm, and I look quickly at the floor.

But James doesn't take the hint to leave, even when I glance at my watch and tap my foot. We stand there facing each other in the hall, which is now completely empty, all the classroom doors shut. I think he's looking at me, but I don't look back. I stare slightly to the left, a strip of his arm and the corner of his T-shirt sleeve, fluttering and dark blue, at the edge of my vision.

"So, you're in our English class now?" James says. "Mr. Jackson can be ridiculous sometimes, but he's not so bad.

Mostly he lets us read what we want to and work with our friends."

I shrug again, cross my arms, and say nothing. I'm not going to leave the school until James isn't looking, and I'm not going to tell him where I'm going.

Finally, he sighs and turns around.

"See you," he mutters, his voice surprising me again. I think he mumbles something else, but I can't make out the words. I don't say anything, and then he's walking away.

As I hit the metal bar in the center of the exit, unlocking it with a thunk that echoes back into the hall, I hunch down under my backpack. I pull it up so it's almost over my head and tell myself no one—not James, not any teachers who might happen to glance my way—can see me.

———

There's not much to look at on the route between school and the hospital. Just houses neatly lined up at a precise distance from the sidewalk, with each one getting smaller the closer they are to the center of town. The trees in people's front yards still wear their summery green even though there's a chill in the air that says fall.

At first, as I walk to a soundtrack of cars and lawnmowers and barking dogs, I try not to think. I study each house as I pass it, whether the colors of the plants outside match the shade of the paint, whether the front door is a staid black or an offbeat purple. I imagine the inside of each house, whether the furniture is antique or square and modern, what colors people picked for their walls and carpets.

Even though I try to distract myself, I check my watch again and again, estimating each time when I'll finally get to the hospital.

But between glances at my wrist, my mind keeps turning back to my conversation with James. I wonder why he was in that hallway at all, why he followed me to ask where I was going. Why Leila told him I was staying at her house.

Before today, James and I have barely spoken for six years.

The last time we did was the first day of sixth grade. In the hallway next to my locker, James and I held our schedules up side by side, the edges of the pages overlapping. No classes together.

"I already checked with Leila," James said. "We're in most of the same ones."

I frowned. I hadn't seen Leila in a few days, since my mother took us out for that drive. When I'd called to ask about her classes, Aunt Cynthia told me Leila was busy getting ready for the first day of school—I pictured her curling her hair with her new curling iron and trying on makeup, which she said everyone started wearing in middle school—and that she'd call me back later. But the only person who called was my mother's social worker, Jeanine, whose "How are you, Sophie?" sounded far too grown-up to be Leila on the other end of the phone. My mother finally made me go to sleep, promising I'd see Leila at school soon enough. But I hadn't found her in the halls that morning either.

The bell rang then, and James and I jumped back as a torrent of people rushed past us. Most of them carried identical bright pink schedules, which flapped where they'd been folded into thirds and stuffed into envelopes. The other sixth graders clutched their schedules tightly; the seventh graders tried to be less obvious about double-checking their classroom numbers on the way to first period.

James and I headed in opposite directions for class, James calling over his shoulder, "See you at lunch, I guess?"

"Okay," I called back, grinning in his direction over other people's heads. I couldn't tell whether he heard me through all the noise.

But when I got to the cafeteria, all the seats around Leila and James were already full. They took up two tables next to each other, with some of the boys James knew from band— the people he hung out with when he wasn't with us—surrounding him, and a few of Leila's louder, peppier friends clustered around her. And then there were people from other elementary schools who I'd never seen before, but who had somehow already found their way to Leila's table, as if she were a magnet pulling them in. I tried to catch her eye, but she didn't look back at me. With her new purple eye shadow and curly hair and her loud laugh, she seemed like a stranger.

As I squeezed past everyone, looking for an empty chair and holding my lunch tray up so it wouldn't spill, Leila's friend Kelly, who was sitting next to her, leaned across the table toward me.

"Hey, Kelly," I said. I stopped with my tray over the head of the girl across from her, hoping one of them would move their bags off the chairs so I could sit down.

"Sophie. Hi," Kelly said. But her voice was stiff, only fake-friendly. I recognized it because it was a voice Leila sometimes used when she was talking to someone she didn't really like. Kelly's eyes flicked away from me, back toward the girl I was standing behind.

I opened my mouth to ask Kelly if I could take the seat next to her. But then she glanced at me again. She lifted up one finger and circled it around her ear, making a few loops—the universal sign for crazy.

She mouthed something to her friend too, but I didn't even try to decipher it. My brain could come up with enough of its own words. Words like wacko. Insane. Bonkers. Even once Kelly stopped, I kept seeing those spirals, her finger circling around her ear, sending me a message. I didn't know whether she was talking about my mother or me, but I was sure she meant one of us.

I stayed where I was, my tray with its square slice of pizza and carton of milk still suspended over everyone's heads, my next breath frozen somewhere in my chest. I waited for Leila or James or anyone to ask Kelly what she was doing or tell her to stop or even just invite me to sit down. But no one said anything.

I called James that afternoon, wanting to ask if he knew why Leila hadn't saved me a seat or returned my calls. But when his mom told me he was at Leila's, I hung up without leaving a message, and he never called back.

NINE

UNTIL I GET TO THE HOSPITAL, I'M HALF CONVINCED MY mother somehow won't be there, or that even if she is, no one will let me see her. But when I tell the gray-haired woman behind the information desk that I'm there to visit "Canon, Amy," she doesn't ask me any questions. She just holds out a pink laminated VISITOR PASS that gives me access to the eighth floor.

"Go right on up, sweetheart," she says, pointing. "Just walk around that corner for the elevator."

I blink when she calls me sweetheart, but I don't say anything. I just put out my hand and take the pass.

———

I walk halfway around the eighth floor, circling the nurses' station twice, before I find my mother's room. A small bronze plaque hangs next to the doorway, and I linger, reading it. *In Memory of Tanya Wilson.*

I trace my index finger along the indented letters, from the bar at the top of the first *I* all the way to the bottom point of the *n*. I wonder vaguely who Tanya Wilson was, why her name is next to this particular door. Did she stay here? Would she be okay with the world knowing that she did?

I don't actually care enough to find out; the wondering is just an excuse not to go inside. Now that I know my mother is here, I don't feel panicked anymore. I'm just anxious and on edge, and I trace my fingers over the letters in Tanya Wilson's name again, going in reverse this time, from the end of the *n* back to the top of the *T.*

But the voice in my head is still whispering its questions, and I know only one way I can get it to leave me alone. So I take one deep breath and one long step. And then I'm in.

———

An empty bed. That's what I see first in the room the receptionist said is my mother's, one extra-long empty bed covered with a single white sheet. I zoom in on it and the panic in my stomach is back. The voice in my head is anxious and loud. *Did they move her but the woman downstairs just didn't know? Or is she really not here at all? Then where is she?*

I force myself to breathe and look up, and that's when I notice the drawn curtain on the other side of the bed, a sheet of yellow fabric that's an old, worn yellow, not a cheerful one. I step over and pull it back, and there's my mother. She's on another bed with plain sheets, covered in layers of white knit blankets. Under them, her legs make two hills. A mini mountain range of mom.

She's sleeping.

I think she's sleeping.

"Mom?" I say, so low she probably wouldn't hear it even if she were awake. I think of yesterday, when I had to check for her breath by putting my ear right over her mouth.

This time I step close to her and stare until I'm certain her chest is moving up and down. Then I take an inventory of the rest of her, from top to bottom, studying her as if I'm going to turn what I see into a sketch. Her hair is still bedraggled and uneven; her face is pale, but not as pale as it was yesterday. Her left arm sits on top of the blankets with an IV attached to it. The IV looks empty, but when I peer at it closely, I see some kind of clear fluid. I watch it trickle down until I realize I'm breathing at the same pace as the drip.

The blankets hide the rest of her body, but I see its outline: her other arm, her hand, her torso. Two legs and two feet. All in order. I want to step closer, to reach out and make sure she's really, solidly there, but I don't want to wake her up or disrupt the careful arrangement of hospital tubes.

So I move back. I'm already reaching behind me for a chair when my legs start to feel wobbly. I fall into the chair instead of sitting, suddenly feeling completely wiped out. But I'm still watching my mother, fascinated by how silent and motionless she is. After how quickly she's been moving and talking for the last week, I'm surprised to see her just sleeping. Like a completely normal person except for the hospital room around us. *Mom*, I want to say, as if the nightmare is actually over, *you scared me.*

I wonder if, whenever she wakes up, she'll be depressed, her voice slow and dull, instead of manic, as if the mysterious inner switch that controls her moods tips when she's asleep. How else could it happen?

At home, I can tell whether my mother is depressed just by looking over to her side of the room when I wake up in the morning. She'll be lying there flat on her back, one arm or maybe a pillow thrown up over her face. She won't whisper to me about breakfast. She won't move, but she'll still radiate something, some kind of invisible Sophie-frequency wave that tells me what kind of day she's about to have: not a good one.

"Mom?" I'll call softly from the doorway on those days. "I'm going to leave for school in a minute. Here's your medicine."

I'll set the glass of water and the plate of pills on her bedside table, following another of the instructions she gave me when I was eleven: *Help me make sure I take my pills,*

Sophie. I'm going to take them, but just in case I forget sometimes, or tell you I don't need them, I want you to remind me. Okay?

Okay.

"Do you want anything for breakfast before I go?" I'll ask. She won't answer. I'll try to keep my voice from sounding impatient, exasperated, even on the days when that's how I feel. I end up sounding the same way I do when I babysit our neighbors' kids, like I'm in charge and pleading with them at the same time. "Mom?"

Sometimes, when I remind her, she'll sit up and take the medicine. Other times, nothing I say gets her to move. I tell her what I just ate and ask her if she'd like some. "If you eat now, you can go back to sleep as soon as you're finished," I say. "I promise when I get home I won't make you tell me what you did all day."

Or I try to joke with her. "My name is Sophie and I'll be your server today. Can I tell you about our specials?"

I offer eggs, toast, cereal, orange juice. Smoothies made from frozen fruit or store-bought waffles warmed in the toaster and covered with syrup. Ice cream with chocolate sprinkles, to see if she's actually paying attention. (I always make sure we have sprinkles, just in case one morning she actually wants some.)

But she never cracks a smile. Sometimes she shakes her head, a slight movement that I catch only because I'm looking for it.

Most of the time, she just lies there. Her arm hangs off the bed as if it's too heavy for her to lift those last few inches. I can't see whatever's weighing her down, but I can almost feel it, a solid presence in the air. Standing there, waiting for her to respond, I start to wonder whether someday I'll be lying there instead.

After a few minutes of trying to get her up, make her laugh, I move over to my side of the room, pick up my bag from the foot of my bed, and swing it on.

"Remember to take your medicine, Mom," I tell her. "I have to leave for school now, or I'll be late. Have a good day."

Please, I think as if I'm praying. *Please take your medicine. Please, please try to have a good day.*

Some of those mornings, she'll finally speak just as I'm leaving the room, her voice coming out gravelly and slow. She'll murmur, "Close the blinds, Sophie, would you." It's a question, but she never manages to bring her voice up at the end.

I ask her if I can leave them open this time. "Maybe the sunlight will make you feel like getting up," I try. But if she answers at all, it's still in that low, slow voice, and she never says yes.

On those mornings, I snap the blinds shut and leave her in the dark.

Then I spend the walk to school reminding myself that she asked me to.

I wake up still in the green vinyl-covered chair next to the hospital bed. I don't remember dozing off, but I'm stretched out, my long legs jutting between the chair and the bed. A nurse is stepping over me to get a closer look at the monitors measuring my mother. It takes me a moment to remember my afternoon: skipping art class, running into James in the hall, walking here.

"Sorry," I say. I sit up quickly. "I think I fell asleep and started to slide off the chair."

The nurse gives me a small smile. "It's not a problem," she says. "That happens pretty often, actually. Those chairs are slippery."

I try, but I don't think my face quite forms a smile back. I'm too nervous. I watch the nurse studying the screens by my mother's bed. She doesn't look particularly concerned, but I decide she's probably trained to act calm all the time, even if things are wrong.

I feel the questions from earlier building up in my head, my chest, my throat, like a cough that's itching to come out, *howwhenwhy*. I feel frantic again with the need to know, even as I tell myself to keep quiet so the nurse can work.

"Is she okay?" I blurt out. Even though the nurse told me yesterday that my mother would be fine, after spending my afternoon imagining the worst, I'm not sure I can believe it anymore. I need to know for sure before I can move on to the more complicated questions about why this happened and whether it will happen again.

The nurse gives me another small smile. "She's stable. Right now we're trying to keep her hydrated, and she's taken a sleeping pill along with her other medication," she says. "The doctor who's been treating her will be in soon. He can answer any other questions you may have about your mother." She, like the nurse yesterday, says *your mother* with a pause, a question mark, checking to make sure she's right. I nod. Are the nurses just guessing when they ask if that's who I am, or do they think I seem like her, tired and numb and straggly haired?

"Thank you," I tell the nurse softly. I tuck my feet under my chair as she moves past it, and she nods at me. Then she tugs the curtain closed behind her and is gone.

———

The doctor does arrive soon, his shiny shoes clicking into the room while I'm still trying to rub the nap out of the corners of my eyes. He has a clipboard folded under his right arm, and I see my mother's name typed across the top. *Canon, Amy.*

"I'm Dr. Choi," he says. His voice sounds exactly the way I imagine it will, solid and mellow. He sticks out a hand. I shake it. "Ms. Canon?"

For a second I think he's talking about my mother, checking if she's the woman in the bed. Then I realize he's just making sure who I am.

"It's Sophie," I say after a too-long pause. "I'm her daughter." Can he see that too?

I tell myself to let him talk before I ask questions. But apparently my mouth has a different plan.

"What happened?" I hear myself asking. But—I picture the pills and the glass of water on the night table again—I know what happened. "I mean, why..."

Dr. Choi backs up to the wall, putting the sole of one shoe flat against the front of the radiator and leaning back against it. He switches feet after a second, and he reminds me of one of those long-legged birds in the videos we saw last year in biology class, balancing in the water.

"You know your mother has bipolar disorder, Sophie," he says, like he's testing me on how much information I already have.

He pauses for me to answer, even though it's not really a question, so I just nod. I remember Aunt Cynthia sitting Leila and me down at her kitchen table and trying to explain what those two words meant, why my mother and I came to stay with Leila, Aunt Cynthia, and Uncle John so often. I think of the books I've read since, sitting on the floor of the 616 aisle at the library in town early on Saturday mornings, when no one else is around, hiding the books under my homework whenever anyone comes around the corner.

"She can have dramatic mood swings if she doesn't take her medication," Dr. Choi says. Another check to see how much I know.

I nod again. "She's been on lithium for the past three years, plus fish oil and vitamins." I rattle off the full list of her medications. It comes out sounding strong and confident, and Dr. Choi blinks at me. He double-checks my mother's chart and his eyes widen like he's impressed.

"We think that's what happened this time," he continues. "That she stopped taking her medication for some reason— maybe she felt she was doing better and therefore didn't need it anymore. Or perhaps she thought it was interfering with her creativity. Many bipolar patients feel that way."

I remember something. "She said her hands were shaking," I tell Dr. Choi. "One day last week, I heard her saying something to herself about how she couldn't control her hands and she was having trouble painting. Maybe she thought it was the medication, so she stopped taking it."

I wait for Dr. Choi to ask me why I didn't follow up, didn't make my mother tell me what she meant about her hands. Why I didn't make sure she kept taking the medication anyway.

I want him to say it, the same thing I've been waiting for

Aunt Cynthia to say since I showed up with my suitcases on her doorstep. That it's my fault.

But Dr. Choi just nods matter-of-factly. He doesn't seem to blame me. In fact, he makes a note on his chart, like maybe what I said was helpful.

"That could very well be what happened," he says. "But once she stopped taking it, she entered what's called a mixed state, where patients experience both manic behavior and depression. Mixed states can be particularly dangerous, because individuals not only often have suicidal thoughts, but also have the energy to carry them out. Or try to."

He says it starkly, the same way I told Leila about my mother getting her stomach pumped. *The energy to carry them out.* Bizarrely, I picture my mother gathering her energy by eating one of those power bars for athletes, then filling up her glass of water at our kitchen sink and carrying it into the bedroom. I imagine her pushing her palm into the cap of the pill bottle and twisting it, lefty loosey, until it snaps off with a loud click. She probably doesn't even notice the sound, or the patter of pills falling into the cap and spilling over onto the bedside table.

But I force my brain to stop there. I don't want to think about what she did next.

I look up at Dr. Choi, who is waiting, watching me, both feet back on the floor, his hands folded over the clipboard at his waist. I'm sure he has a million other patients to see, but he doesn't glance at his watch. He looks like he doesn't have anything else he needs to be doing.

Part of me wants to say what I'm still sure he's thinking. *It was my fault. I should have known she wasn't taking her medication, after I promised I'd remind her. I should have found that other bottle of pills before she had a chance to use it.* As if admitting all of that myself would somehow get my mother off the hook, get Dr. Choi to say *oh, of course it wasn't her fault, let's send her home right now.* Maybe it would erase those sympathetic looks from Dr. Choi's and the nurses' faces; the expressions that make guilt squirm around in my stomach.

But another part of me doesn't want to confess until I get some answers too. It wants to ask how my mother could do this, knowing I would be the one to find her. Whether she realized that what she planned to do would mean leaving me alone, or whether she thought of me at all.

I don't know which of those things I want to be the truth.

I also realize none of these are questions Dr. Choi can answer. So I tell myself it's fine, it's enough, that I know the facts.

"Okay," I say. I nod again to show I've processed everything he's told me, the good student my mother always thinks I am. And to give myself an extra second so my voice will come out steady. "What happens now?"

TEN

I SAY IT INTO THE SILENCE OF THE DINNER TABLE, WHERE Aunt Cynthia and Uncle John have run out of stories to tell about their workdays. Leila asked what I thought about English class and Mr. Jackson, but I didn't want to say any of the things that popped into my head, about how weird it was to be in class with her and James again and how I spent the entire period remembering yesterday afternoon, so I shrugged and didn't answer. Now, next to me, Leila's just silently bolting down her chicken before she leaves for band rehearsal.

While I speak, I keep my eyes on my food: a chicken drumstick with sauce and piles of rice and salad and snow peas.

"I saw my mother's doctor today," I tell my plate. The pink and black triangles edging the white china look like

70

teeth, and I imagine them opening up and talking back. Someone's fork clangs loudly against a dish.

When I look up, Uncle John meets my eyes, and I feel Leila looking at me from my right. Only Aunt Cynthia stares down at the table.

I start talking again, wincing when my voice croaks.

"The doctor said he thinks she'll need to spend about ten days in the hospital. Maybe as long as two weeks. She'll need more treatment after that, but the doctors will have to decide whether to recommend her for an outpatient or a residential program based on how she's doing."

I look up. Now they're all looking back at me.

I hurry through the rest of what Dr. Choi told me. "The hospital stay is just to get her stabilized, but the doctors will have to see how she's doing on the new medication before they decide what kind of treatment to recommend next."

My words are exactly the ones Dr. Choi used. *Stabilized, treatment, facility, evaluate.* I sound like a medical textbook, but I almost like the terms. They sound concrete enough to hold, but when I say them, I don't feel like I'm talking about my mother.

I see Leila out of the corner of my eye, and the expression on her face looks almost sympathetic, her mouth slightly turned down and her eyes sad. But that can't be.

No one else says anything. I spear a snow pea with my

fork and chew it slowly, listening to the crunch reverberate inside my head.

A throat clears.

"You can stay here for as long as it takes," Aunt Cynthia says.

I'm so surprised to hear her speak that I look up again, and our eyes meet, accidentally, for just a second.

"It sometimes takes longer than the doctors say it will, so I just wanted to say that." She trails off.

I stare. My empty fork points toward my mouth.

That's all she has to say?

My mother is her sister too.

Uncle John must see something in my face, because he leans forward and jumps in before Aunt Cynthia can say more.

"We'll know more in two weeks" are his words. His tone says *calm down, everyone.*

"But that's what I'm saying, John," Aunt Cynthia interrupts, not hearing what he's trying to say. "Sometimes it takes longer, and I don't want Sophie to feel—"

Leila pushes her chair away from the table with a sudden scraping sound that makes the rest of us jump and Aunt Cynthia stop talking. I don't look up as her boots clomp over to the garbage and her fork shoves the last of the food off her plate. The dish clinks into the sink.

"I have to leave for rehearsal," Leila says. Her boots move from the sink to the doorway. "I'll be home late."

The rest of us stay quiet as Leila moves through the living room and the front hall, as the door closes behind her. I picture her on the other side, looking down the steps to the lawn, her car in the driveway, the opposite of the view I had yesterday. If the scene were a photograph, what would her caption be?

I push my own chair back from the table and stand up with only one more quick glance at Aunt Cynthia and Uncle John. Like Leila, I dump the last of my food into the trash and my plate into the sink. As I follow my cousin's path out of the room, I hear my aunt's and uncle's voices fill the silence behind me, soft but rising.

———

I'm in the guest room—my room—finishing the last of my math homework when I hear the knock at my door. Three soft taps, then whoever's on the other side clears his throat and taps a fourth time.

"Come in," I call. The words are too quiet and I have to repeat them before I hear the knob turn. In the chair behind the tiny wooden desk, I shift so I can see the doorway. My legs jut out to the side and I jiggle my feet. The chair creaks under me.

Uncle John steps into the room, meets my eyes, then

looks at the floor. He takes a seat at the end of the bed, elbows on his knees and wrists hanging down. I remember the way he used to be, teasing Leila and me, trying to make us laugh. He seems so serious now.

"You have to understand that this is stressful for your aunt too," he says.

I do?

"She is worried about Amy. She just wanted to make sure you know you're welcome here."

I shrug. I'm not sure I care what she was trying to do, and I don't really want to listen to Uncle John taking her side.

"But that's not actually what I came up here to talk to you about," he says.

I stop moving my feet, and under me, the chair stops creaking.

"How would you feel about a job in my office after school?" Uncle John asks.

I look up. That wasn't what I expected him to say. Was this what he and Aunt Cynthia were talking about in the kitchen after I followed Leila out?

"I was thinking maybe two afternoons a week and Saturdays," he says. "We could use your art and math skills, and we pay our part-time employees by the hour."

Ah.

Uncle John and Aunt Cynthia must know how much my

mother's time in the hospital will cost us. This must be their way of offering to help.

I look at the floor again, wondering what my mother would say. Would she wave Uncle John off with a laugh, tell him she'd come up with some other way to get the money? Would she be angry or offended? Would she agree and promise to pay him back later, everyone knowing but not saying that that would never happen?

I wish for her, a sharp thought that leaves an ache behind, like the smoke from a blown-out candle after a birthday wish.

I imagine her sitting in this chair, having this conversation with Uncle John, and that's when I know: she would refuse the money. She'd be convinced the two of us could manage on our own. But I also know Uncle John is right. My mother's illness and her irregular job mean she can't get good insurance. I think of the way I divide our money every week—anything she's gotten from selling a painting, whatever the neighbors have given me to watch their kids for a few hours after school—to pay for our groceries, the rent on our apartment, her medication.

There usually isn't anything left over.

"Okay," I say. "That would be helpful."

It doesn't feel like I've said enough.

"Thank you," I add after a pause.

The words come out sounding formal rather than grateful, but Uncle John doesn't seem to expect anything else. He nods and stands up.

"We can start tomorrow," he says gently. He pulls the door closed behind him.

ELEVEN

WHEN THE ALARM RINGS EARLY THE NEXT MORNING, Saturday, I open my eyes to see the bright red numbers on the clock glaring at me as if they're as angry about the time as I am. I slam the heel of my hand against the snooze button and turn over, cocooning myself in the pale guest room sheets. I don't fall back asleep. I just work my fingers into the weave of the blanket, pulling it out of shape. Soon there's a thumb-sized hole in the cream-colored knit.

At home I get up as soon as the alarm rings because I'm afraid the noise will bother my mother, lying in her bed on the other side of the room. The times she actually goes to sleep, I don't want anything to wake her up before she's rested. But this morning I hit snooze again and again and again. I'm half hoping it will wake up everyone else in the house.

Until eventually even I'm sick of the alarm's *enh-enh-enh*, and I shut it off and unroll myself from the blankets. When I trudge downstairs and into the kitchen in my pajamas, Leila's already there. And she doesn't look like my blaring alarm woke her up. She's dressed and the counter is strewn with ingredients. As I stand in the doorway, she levels off a cup of flour from a canister and dumps it into a mixing bowl.

She turns and sees me. "Morning," she says, almost cheerfully, like we've always lived in the same house and greeted each other at breakfast.

I don't say anything, and after a minute of prickly silence and another cup of flour, Leila speaks again.

"I was late to rehearsal last night, so I got stuck having to bake for the whole band."

Late because I kept everyone at the dinner table to talk about my mother? But Leila doesn't say that.

I step into the kitchen, the floor creaking under my bare feet, as if I can somehow step into this, an actual conversation with my cousin. "What happens if you don't bake for everyone?"

Leila adds sugar to the mixture in her bowl, cracks an egg rhythmically against the side.

"I have to sing in the hallway at school, between every period, for a whole day. That's James's rule."

"And that's worse?"

Leila looks at me, a look that says *of course*. The Leila in my head is loud, willing to be wild, up for anything. I've forgotten that the real Leila can be just as cautious as I am.

"James probably just wanted the free food," I say, even though I'm not sure I know James that well anymore. "He wouldn't have made you sing."

"Of course not," Leila agrees with me. "But I wanted cookies anyway. This is just an excuse. Actually, the whole singing thing reminded me of those notes your mom used to give you—you know the ones where she'd tell you to pretend to be someone else for the day? I'm surprised she never told you to be a singer."

I nod mutely, but Leila can't see me, because she's busy fiddling with the measuring cups on the counter. There's a lump in my stomach and I have no idea what to say. Leila and I don't talk about my mother.

Leila has no idea my mother still gives me those notes.

"Here," Leila says abruptly, pulling a mixer out of its box on the counter. "Hold this." The real Leila has no trouble ordering me around. That's something she shares with the Leila in my head.

I could say no, but I actually like being asked, having something to do with my hands. So I take the mixer from her and stick the beaters in, pushing until they click into their slots.

"I need to add these in while the mixer's going," Leila says, pointing to more measuring cups full of chocolate chips and coconut. "So whenever you're ready…"

I plug the mixer in and stretch the cord back across the counter to the bowl. Leila reaches over with the cup of chocolate chips. I switch the mixer on and stick it in the bowl—and cookie dough flies *everywhere*. The counter, our clothes, the floor, our hair.

We both shriek and jump back. Leila curses, I try to hold the mixer in the bowl and find the off switch while also keeping my pajamas away from the airborne flour-sugar-egg mixture, and somewhere in there the doorbell rings. For a minute there's a rhythm, the bell's *ding-dong*, *ding-dong* combined with the whir of the mixer.

Then, at once, everything is quiet. Dough is crumbling off the ends of my hair and I still have my arm stretched over the bowl, holding the turned-off mixer and trying to contain the damage. A drop of dough with a chocolate chip in it falls from Leila's sleeve onto the counter and her shoulders slump. I've just ruined her recipe.

I want to pick up the bowl and chuck all of the dough into the trash. How can Leila calmly and neatly bake a batch of cookies while I, even though I cook meals at home almost every day, can't manage a simple mixer?

But Leila isn't angry. I hear a soft sound coming from her,

and when I look over, I realize she's actually *laughing*. So hard her shoulders are shaking and she can barely catch her breath.

"You have to...tilt the bowl...to keep everything from flying around," she manages to say, bossy again.

Without warning, she picks a glob of dough off her shirt and flings it at me, hard, right at my nose. I duck, but it still hits the top of my head, adding to the sticky mess in my hair.

I'm holding some dough myself, about to pelt it back at her, when Uncle John walks into the kitchen, followed by James, his hair falling over his face.

"Look who I found at the front door," Uncle John announces. Then he sees the mess.

Behind him, James's eyes meet mine, and then they travel over my dough-covered hair and pajamas. James grins and raises an eyebrow, and I feel myself start to turn red. I drop the handful of cookie dough I was about to toss at Leila back into the mixing bowl. James follows my arms to the bowl and his eyes light up, a mischievous look I recognize even though the face that's making it is five years older.

Leila and I, knowing what's coming next, reach for the bowl at the same time. She gets to it first and hugs it toward her, heedless of the flour and sugar lining its edge.

"No," she tells James forcefully, still clutching the bowl and walking sideways with it toward the sink. He reaches over the counter for it, she holds it away, and both of them start laughing.

James catches my eyes over Leila's head, and I smile, thinking that this feels almost the way it used to.

But then Uncle John interrupts. "We can head out whenever you're ready, Sophie," he says, and his words pull me away from the scene in the kitchen. They zoom me out of the room and up, up, until I'm back in the guest room by myself, no longer in on the joke.

TWELVE

AS WE DRIVE TO HIS OFFICE ONE TOWN OVER, UNCLE John talks about the projects he'll be meeting with clients about today. Every so often, he interrupts himself to point out houses his firm worked on. Some are still under construction, wooden frames up where new rooms will go. I try to pay attention, to imagine the houses those frames will become, but the car's motion lulls me, and soon my mind starts to wander.

My mother loves to drive around and look at houses. Her favorite is one about forty-five minutes away from our town, out in a more rural part of New Jersey near farms and apple orchards. But it isn't a farmhouse. It's more modern than all the other homes, all glass and pale wood, towering over the nearby trees.

Sometimes she'd drive us out there in our rattling green

car and park in front of the house, turning the engine off but making no move to get out.

"Mom," I'd say, sometimes lowering my voice to a whisper, as if the people in the house could hear us through the car windows and across the lawn. "What are you doing? I bet they're wondering who we are, sitting out here. We're probably making them nervous. What if they come out and ask us what we want?"

The sunlight reflecting off the glass panes on the front of the house made it hard to look inside. But sometimes, if I squinted, I could see people moving around. Their furniture looked like the frame of the house, stark and plain and uncomfortable. Out back was another structure that looked like a mini house on stilts, with a window that stretched all the way across one wall.

"Come on, Sophie," my mother would say, in that tone that meant *do you really have to be so uptight all the time?*

Why don't you bring Leila, then, if you want someone who will be more fun? I would always argue back in my head. But I never said it.

"It's just for a few minutes," my mother would say, cajoling me. "I'm sure they don't mind at all. They can't have a house like this, out here with all this farmland, and not expect people to stop and look at it. We always see other people stopping to take pictures."

Then she would turn slightly, to face the house and me. "Now, tell me," she would say. She'd pat the corner of her seat as if inviting me to come closer and share a secret, and I always wanted to lean over and give her a hug at that moment. "When we live in this house, which room do you want to have?" She would nod toward the second floor, where I could look through the windows into a few of the rooms. I could see a pillow against a wall, the corner of a dresser, the knob on an open closet door.

While I wondered who lived in each room, my mother would open her arms and laugh.

"Sophie, you know what? When we live here, you can have as many rooms as you want! One to sleep in, one to brush your hair in, one to keep shoes in, one to sketch in. Anything!"

Then she would point toward the structure behind the house, another thing she always did. "Except for that," she would say, nodding decisively. "That's going to be my studio. Much better light than the basement. I bet whoever built that is an artist."

That's when I would stop her. "Mom, why are we even talking about this? We're never going to live in this house."

It seemed so unlikely I didn't want to imagine it. I made myself think of our tiny, shabby apartment instead, of counting out the money for groceries and my mother's medication every Friday afternoon after school. Of how, whenever my mother sold a painting for more than she expected, she used the money up almost as soon as she got it. Sometimes she couldn't even remember the next day what she'd spent it on. An evening gown she wouldn't wear, a piece of jewelry for me that was far too fancy for school, an expensive rug that might have paint on it within a few days. How could we possibly afford to have this house? We never could, unless we won the lottery. My mother bought lottery tickets all the time, fanning them out across the kitchen table and comparing each winning number to the list in the newspaper. But I knew how small the odds of winning were.

My mother would put the car back in drive then and pull away from the curb. I would glance quickly over my shoulder for traffic, because my mother always forgot to check her mirrors. I never saw anything, but sometimes a horn blared from behind us and another car would speed by. The road was always wide and empty, so it was easy for the person honking to swerve around our car. But I wondered what the other driver was thinking, whether he muttered *crazy lady* as he passed my mother, who drove without looking while talking about life in a house that wasn't hers.

"You never know, Sophie," my mother would say as we drove away. She sounded disappointed at my lack of imagination, and I told myself that next time I would talk about the house with her the way she wanted me to. I would pick a bedroom and everything. "Things could change."

———

"Well, here we are," Uncle John says, shutting the car off. I unbuckle my seat belt and open my door, shaking off the memory.

I already have such a clear picture of Uncle John's office in my mind—a small house with bright yellow siding and a narrow strip of parking lot off to one side; a room full of wide wooden desks that Leila and I hid under with drawing paper one year on Take Your Child to Work Day—that I have to blink a few times to convince myself that's not actually where we are.

We're parked in a field, not a lot. There are no desks here, no rugs across wooden floors, no framed photos from design magazines hanging on the walls with captions trumpeting *comfort* and *relaxation*. There's tall grass around us, four other cars, a few people in work boots carrying notepads and folders and pencils.

When I follow Uncle John out of the car, I see why. The field isn't just a field. At the other end is a house, small and slanting. We're looking at it from the side, and one of the windows, partially punched out, stares back at us, gaping. The front porch looks intact, but the wood of the back porch tilts downward toward the ground.

Uncle John leads me to a tall table in front of the house.

"Claire," Uncle John calls, and a woman steps away from the table. "This is my niece, Sophie. Sophie, this is Claire Greenberg, our newest project manager."

"Nice to meet you," Claire says, sticking out a hand for me to shake. She's polite, but she seems frazzled, still half-turned toward the table. "Natalie's around the back taking photos," she tells Uncle John.

We start walking again, following a path of trampled grass around the side of the house. It feels like the windows are peering down at us, curious and wary.

"The people who own this land"—Uncle John waves his arm toward the house and its overgrown yard—"just hired us to build something here. They think they want to keep at least part of the existing structure, so we could use some sketches of it."

"Okay," I say, pulling my sketchbook and a pencil from my bag as we go. I'm not sure why the photos won't be enough, but I agreed to come here, so I'll do whatever Uncle John asks me to.

We round the back corner of the house and there's a girl my age in front of us, pointing a camera toward the back porch. I recognize her by the blue streak in her hair, Natalie from my art class. She stands squarely on the grass in her laced-up boots and dress, the kind of outfit I don't remember seeing her wear before this year. Something about her posture says she doesn't want to be here either.

"Natalie is Claire's daughter," Uncle John explains, which I should have realized when Claire said her last name. "Claire recently got divorced, so on weekends when Natalie's younger sister is with their dad, Natalie usually helps us out around the office or on projects."

So all the relatives no one knows what to do with get stuck here.

Uncle John and I walk toward Natalie, who's staring at the back of her camera and hasn't seen us yet. She shifts her weight and holds the camera to her eye, fiddling with a setting.

"Natalie!" Uncle John shouts, and she looks up. I can tell she recognizes me, even though there's nothing memorable about me, no boots or dyed hair.

"Hey," she says, cordial but not exactly warm.

I nod back. I can do cordial.

I settle into the grass as Uncle John leaves, opening my sketchbook onto my lap. I work quickly, getting the slanted porch, the paint-flecked door, the all-seeing windows onto the page. I hear an occasional click as Natalie moves around me, shooting the house from all angles.

I'm halfway through my sketch by the time she kneels down next to me.

"So you're the other pity intern," she says.

I nod again. That's it exactly.

"Welcome to the club."

It's still not quite friendly, but Natalie doesn't walk away again. Instead she sits fully on the grass. She angles the camera, and her index finger, with its dark nail polish chipping off the nail, clicks the button rapidly, once, twice, three times. I can't see the photo on the back of the camera, only the light that flickers from the images as she quickly reviews each one.

"I think my mom is convinced that if she doesn't bring me here, I'll mope in my room all weekend. Or run away to the city or something," she says, still looking intently at the back of her camera.

"Would you?" I ask.

I try to remember what I've thought of her before, whether she seems like the kind of person who would run away, but I have no idea. In my memory there are only a few images of her, walking through the halls, sitting in art class looking through one of Ms. Triste's books.

Natalie shrugs.

"I don't know. My boyfriend is there. And my dad, now."

She sounds uncertain, defeated, somehow, by the fact that she has to be here and not there. I try to imagine what Natalie's boyfriend might be like. I picture someone with giant headphones on, listening to indie music, wearing a T-shirt no one else understands.

I see her peering at my sketchbook, and I turn it slightly toward her, so she can watch me shade in the next section of my drawing.

"That's really good," she says. "No wonder you can skip art."

I look over at her. I'm not sure how to begin to explain that I wasn't just cutting class or why I stayed in the hall to talk to James or the fact that I walked right out of school and to the hospital to see my mother.

"My turn," I say instead, reaching out a hand for her camera. "Let me see."

Natalie presses a button for me and I see her first picture. I'm not a photographer, but I know these can't be the kinds of photos Claire and Uncle John were looking for. Wherever Natalie was standing, the sun was at exactly the right angle to whiten the shot. In another photo, I see the edge of a finger poking into the photo's frame.

But I keep clicking through, and as I do, the photos start to get good, as if Natalie couldn't quite keep herself from caring or from using everything she knew about how to compose an image. There's one I stop on. Natalie must have taken it from a distance, at least as far back as where Uncle John parked the car, and maybe from up on a hill. The building looks so small, almost lost in its own overgrown lawn. It could be an illustration for a picture book. *"What will happen to me?" asks the empty house.*

"This one's incredible," I tell Natalie, turning the camera so she can see which one I mean. She's flopped backward onto the lawn, and I lie down too, letting the grass tickle all the parts of me it can reach.

I hold the camera screen above both of us, and Natalie explains how she composed a few of the photos as I click through them. Like her photos, better with each shot, her voice gets more animated as we talk, until she's moving her arms and everything. She almost whacks my face with one enthusiastic gesture.

"Sorry," she says, and we get quiet again. I've made it through all of her photos and am back at those first few, the intentionally bad ones.

"So why is your dad dragging you here?" Natalie asks after a few minutes.

I'm confused. *My dad?* Then I realize who she's talking about.

"Oh, John's my uncle," I say. "Not my dad. I'm staying with them right now—my uncle and his family." That doesn't sound quite right. "My aunt and her family, actually." I correct myself again. *"My family."*

"Sounds complicated," Natalie says.

92

I laugh a little.

"Yeah," I say. Natalie doesn't pry.

We lie there on the lawn quietly, almost covered by grass and weeds. I pass the camera back to Natalie, pull up a few weeds, and braid them together. This silence doesn't feel full of all the things we're not saying, the way sitting in the car with Leila does. With Leila or James, with Aunt Cynthia or Uncle John, I never explain myself either, but this is the first time I feel like I don't have to.

Next to me, Natalie points her camera randomly and clicks, trying to take interesting shots by accident. By the time Uncle John comes looking for me, I've woven a whole grassy crown, and I set it down by Natalie's head. She turns her camera toward it.

"See you Monday," she says.

"Yeah," I say as I stand up. "See you Monday."

———

When I walk into my mother's hospital room the next day, I don't have to study her for signs she's breathing. She's sitting up, staring at a tray of hospital food on the rolling table that extends over her lap. She isn't eating anything, and I can understand why. The meat—I think it's meat—is floating in an unidentifiable brown gravy, and the dessert, some kind of cake with a layer of "fruit" that might be jam, looks like it's trying to wriggle its way off the plate.

"Mom, hi," I say. "It's me."

She lifts her head, refocuses her eyes on my face.

"Hello, Sophie," she says. She doesn't sound happy to see me. Her voice has no expression at all. It's flat and slow, like it's about to run out of batteries.

I speak more quickly, as if that will somehow make her do the same. "Are you done with that? Why don't I get it out of your way?"

I slide the rolling table down the bed and into the corner. I don't think my mother actually cares, but I don't want to look at the mystery meat and wobbly dessert if I don't have to.

"How are you feeling today, Mom? Have you eaten? Has the doctor been by?" I hear my own voice coming out louder than it usually does, even though I know my mother can hear me perfectly well. I take a seat next to the bed, slinging my backpack off onto the floor. I lean in.

My mother lifts her shoulders, managing half a shrug, and then a half-shake of her head. "Tired," she says. "My head feels cloudy. Full of fuzz. Can't think clearly."

I nod. "Dr. Choi said this would happen, remember?"

I don't mean to talk to her like she's a child, but that's how my voice comes out. Basic words, small sentences, loud and lifting up brightly at the end.

"It's the medication making you feel like that. Some of the side effects will wear off once you get used to it, or the

94

doctors will try you on something else." I say it like it's easy: one medication doesn't work, that's okay, there's another one we can try. Even though I know it's not so simple.

I stand up. "Do you want to go down the hall to the lounge and play a board game with me for a little while? Or I have a deck of cards in here." I reach down for my bag and pull out the small cardboard box I found in Aunt Cynthia's guest room.

But my mother slowly drags her head from one side to the other. No, no board game or cards. She doesn't want the TV on either.

I suggest every activity I can think of. Sketching, listening to the radio. I could go downstairs to the cafeteria and pick up a snack. Maybe some fruit? Something healthier than the dinner she didn't eat. But my mother just keeps shaking her head. No, no, and no.

And for a second, just one second, I want to shake her, to lean in close to her ear and shout until she snaps out of it. Even though I know from years of watching her that her depressions aren't the kind of thing a person can snap out of, I still want to yell. *Hello, it's me! Remember me? Your daughter? That person who lives with you and takes care of you and who you completely forgot about the other day when you decided to try to—oh yeah—kill yourself?* In my head the words get louder, until I'm sure my mother can hear them somehow.

But I hold them all in, pushing the words back behind that rusty door in my head with as much force as I can. The anger tries to batter its way out again, but I imagine myself leaning against the door hard, forcing it to stay shut. I take a deep breath.

Then I pick up the TV remote and flip through channels until I find a baseball game, one that looks like it's just starting and will be on for hours. I have no idea who's playing. I leave it on mute.

"You might want something to look at later tonight," I tell my mother, nodding toward the TV and hoping I sound calmer than I feel. "But maybe we can play cards next time."

I lean back in the bedside chair. Instead of shuffling the deck of cards, I reach for my sketchbook and flip it open to the next empty page, right after my sketches of the abandoned house.

I don't usually like to draw people. But when I start sketching, what comes out is my mother's outline, the hill of legs under the blanket, the long hair, the upturned hand. I break her body down into abstract shapes as I draw them with fierce strokes. They're just circles and ovals and lines, but together they look something like the person lying in front of me.

When I pull my hand back and look at what I've drawn, something about my lines makes it look like the figure on the paper is living, breathing, moving. Like my mother could step off the page, laughing, and start telling me a story about her day. The pencil strokes are more animated than the woman lying in bed in front of me.

But when I blink and open my eyes again, the lines are just streaks on the page, still and gray.

THIRTEEN

MONDAY MORNING, AND LEILA HAS THE RADIO TUNED, blasting, to a song I hate. At the dinner table we manage to speak to each other politely when Aunt Cynthia and Uncle John start conversations, everyone making small talk about school, work, band, homework. But in the car I feel like a tiny country at the mercy of a superpower armed with ear-piercing music. I'm the losing side in a cold war. There are no more polite questions about my mother, just noise that screams *I'm ignoring you* as loudly as anything can. Today the screaming actually matches the noise in my head, an echo of everything I wanted to yell at my mother yesterday.

I want to put my hands over my ears and curl up into the small space between the seat and the door. But I refuse to let Leila know her music is bothering me. So

I sit there, stiff and silent, while she sings along and bobs her head.

Then the sound suddenly gets much softer and Leila is speaking next to me.

"Hey there," she says cheerfully.

I look over. Is she actually talking to me now?

But no. Her silver cell phone is next to her ear, pinched between her cheek and her shoulder while she steers. I would have expected her to let go of the wheel to hold the phone, but she still has both hands planted in place at ten and two.

"Oh no, sweetie," she says into the phone, her voice losing its chipper edge. "I'm so sorry."

I wonder who Leila's talking to. She doesn't look over at me, and I assume she's forgotten I'm even in the car. For a moment I wonder if something's really wrong.

"Did something happen?" Leila asks into the phone. "How long are they grounding you for?"

Oh.

It must be one of Leila's friends, in trouble for something. I roll my eyes out the window so Leila won't be able to see, watching my own pupils move up and over in my reflection. Then I pretend to be staring intently at my phone while I turn the ringer off for school.

Leila makes soft *mhmm* and *oh* and *I'm sorry* noises into

99

the phone as she drives. I spend the time wondering who's on the other end and why Leila is the one she calls when she needs to talk first thing in the morning.

"I'll give you a ride home after school," Leila says, like she's answering a question, and then silence. She must've ended the call. When I look over, Leila's hand is already hovering over the radio dial, ready to turn it up again, the phone back in its usual spot in the cup holder. I'm convinced I could have opened my door and gotten out at the last light without her even noticing.

Until Leila glances at me and starts to talk.

"That was Liz," she says, as if I know and care who Liz is. "She got in trouble with her parents and her punishment is not being allowed to practice with us for three weeks."

Liz must be someone in James and Leila's band. I want to roll my eyes out the window again. Why do I care?

I think suddenly of one evening the summer before sixth grade, when Leila called me just before bed the way she always did. This time she had something different to tell me: that she had a crush on one of our classmates, a boy named Steven who had been at the park all summer when we were there with my mother.

"Will you talk to him for me?" she asked.

I said okay, but I wasn't really sure what she meant. "What do I say?"

"Just ask him if he likes me too. I'll talk to someone for you! Who do you like?"

I lowered my voice in case my mom could hear from the kitchen, but I didn't hesitate before telling Leila the name. "James," I whispered, my face turning red even though Leila couldn't see me. I twisted the phone cord in my fingers, nervous about what she would say. He was her friend too, so was it okay for me to like him not just as our friend?

"Really?" Leila had started to whisper too. Then she giggled a little, and I knew she didn't mind. "Okay, I'll talk to him for you."

It was so easy to tell her anything then. But now, here in the car, I have no idea what to say to her. I don't even know who Liz is. Between my mother and Leila and James and Aunt Cynthia and Uncle John and school and work, I can't find space in my head for anyone else. So I just lean my head against the cold window and stay silent until the car pulls in at school.

In *English, Mr. Jackson, Room 210*, Mr. Jackson has forgotten that I wasn't there for the first few days of class, and he's stopped interrupting himself to tell me about assignments he already explained to everyone else. I sit in my corner seat with my notebook open, scribbling something every few minutes so it looks like I'm paying attention. But really I'm just filling the margins with doodles, my hand weaving randomly down the page.

I did the reading for class yesterday while sitting by my mother's bed. But I kept losing my place, hearing the nurses' shoes squeak down the hall or a patient making noise in another room, and I barely remember anything I read. So while Mr. Jackson asks questions about character and symbolism, I just sit there, not raising my hand, not looking up, only half listening. I tune out completely once someone in front of me starts reading aloud from the book. I don't know the boy's name, he sounds bored, and I can't concentrate on his voice. When I let my eyes wander around the classroom, I catch James's gaze once. His mouth moves like maybe he's trying to talk to me, but I can't understand what he's saying, so I just look back at my notebook. The memory from the car this morning pops back into my head, and I wonder whether Leila ever talked to him, back in sixth grade, like she said she would. Is that why he didn't call me back?

I snap back to the present only when I hear chairs scraping the floor all around me. The bell hasn't rung yet, but when I look up everyone is moving, switching seats, shifting desks around. When the noise stops, most people are in clumps of three or four. Mr. Jackson picks up the thick books that are stacked on the back table and starts to hand them out. I look at the cover. It's a giant anthology of poetry.

"Sophie," Mr. Jackson calls. I snap my head up, wondering if he can somehow tell how uninterested I am in this book.

But that's not it: one of my classmates is standing to my right, and I realize he's waiting to take my desk, which sits slightly apart from all the others.

"Don't you have a group?" Mr. Jackson asks. "Everyone needs to work in groups of three or four on this next project."

I try not to roll my eyes, but it doesn't matter, because Mr. Jackson is already looking away from me, scanning the room for a cluster with an empty spot. I'm sure everyone's looking at me, the one person without any friends in the class to form a group with. I want to slide down in my seat until I'm hidden behind my desk, or until Mr. Jackson forgets I'm there at all, whichever happens first. I'm afraid everyone can see how confused I am, how disconnected I feel from everything: the readings, the questions, Mr. Jackson's group work. All those thoughts feel fuzzy around the edges. The only ones that penetrate the fog are the worries about my mother; the questions from the voice in my head, wondering how she's doing.

"Oh, here we are," Mr. Jackson says. "There's one group of two, so grab your stuff and come on over." He says the last part loudly, like an enthusiastic game show host.

Come…on…over! Everyone looks our way, and a few people laugh.

I stand up, poetry book heavy in my hand, and look across the room to the empty desk. On either side of it sit—out of everyone in the class—Leila and James.

Of course.

They have their heads bent over Leila's notebook, where they're taking turns writing something, but they look up at the sudden silence in the room. When she sees me, Leila looks the way I feel—dismayed. James just watches me, and I have no idea, still, how to read the expression on his face. A small part of me wants to laugh because this, of all things, is happening to me right now. The rest of me wants to turn around and sit down again at my own desk, take a zero on the assignment, hand in the giant book of poems I already know I don't care about reading. I'd rather be in math class, where at least each answer makes me feel like I'm getting closer to understanding, solving, something. Or chemistry, where I can measure and balance. Here, with poetry and novels and vocabulary, I just feel impatient.

But the screeching noise I hear behind me, the sound of metal chair legs against floor tiles, tells me my own desk has already been co-opted for someone else's group. I can't spend the rest of the period standing in the middle of the classroom, so I cross the space and take a seat in the third desk of James and Leila's cluster. James turns toward me and nods without saying anything, then ducks his head. Leila stares down at her notebook as if whatever she and James were writing there is absolutely the most important thing she'll ever read anywhere.

Whatever this group project is, I already have a feeling it isn't going to go well.

At the front of the room, Mr. Jackson clears his throat.

"Well then, now that everyone is in groups, let's get down to business. Your assignment is this: choose one poem in the book that everyone in your group likes, maybe something that you all find meaningful for your own reasons. Then work together to research the life of the poet and come up with a creative project that represents the poem or the poet's life in some way."

I zone out while Mr. Jackson describes some of the projects students did last year. When I tune back in, he's finishing up the instructions.

"The key word here is *creative*," he says. "You can turn in written reports if that's really what your group wants to do, but please try to do something a little more visually interesting. A poster, a diorama. You can even dress up in costume if you want to." Everyone laughs, not sure whether he's serious. I glance at James and see a faint smile on his face. I wonder if he's imagining, like I am, what it would be like if the three of us showed up to class dressed as something from a poem. I picture Leila in costume as a flower or a cloud, then start to sketch it in a cartoon style in the corner of my notebook.

Mr. Jackson looks up at the clock over the door. "The bell's about to ring, so before you all peace out"—more laughs—"please set up a time to meet with your groups outside of class to get started. We've got a lot to get through with the poetry unit, so we won't have much class time to work on these. I'll send around the presentation sign-up sheet tomorrow."

All around us, as Mr. Jackson settles behind his desk, people whip out calendars and phones and start comparing dates. At our desk cluster, no one says anything. None of us actually wants to have a meeting outside of class.

"How about Wednesday night?" James finally says. His not-a-little-kid voice surprises me again, and I wonder if that will ever stop happening. "I know we don't have jazz band that night, and we could do it after my shift ends at work. Sophie, are you free?"

I nod. The words *I'll just need to visit my mother in the hospital* are right there on the tip of my tongue. But I don't let them slide off.

"Okay, how about eight o'clock?" James says. "We could have pizza?"

We all nod, still not meeting each other's eyes.

The bell rings and Leila stands up so fast her whole desk moves, screeching across the floor.

"Let's do it at my house, since two of us are there right now, anyway," she says.

And then she spins and walks out, kicking her chair on the way, without giving us a chance to respond.

"O-kay," James says softly once she's gone, and I look at him. Just for a moment, I forget about James and Leila chatting in the parking lot and writing in her notebook, about James showing up at the house to meet Leila for rehearsal, and it feels the same way it did when we were kids, Leila giving the orders and leaving the two of us to carry them out, her loyal foot soldiers. James rolls his eyes and a sort of resigned smile flashes across his face. I smile back, as if we're on the playground again, refusing to chase the ball when it's really Leila's turn to do it.

"What do you think?" James asks me. "Costumes?" He flips his own notebook toward me, showing me a drawing of three stick figures in what look like togas.

I laugh.

The sound rings out, startling me so much I clap my hand over my mouth as if I'm trying to keep it from happening again. I turn the corner of my notebook toward him so he can see my drawings of Leila as a flower and a cloud.

He grins. "That's much better than mine. Good thing you're the artist," he says, like he just knows I still am.

Then we both stand up and gather our books. I follow James into the hallway. But we turn in separate directions, and the feeling of having an ally again disappears as I walk away.

When I open the door to the art room, I'm surprised by how happy Ms. Triste is to see me. She rushes toward the door, a broad smile on her face.

"Sophie! Welcome back. I thought you would be joining us on Friday, but it's wonderful to see you today."

I mumble something about my schedule getting changed, even though it has nothing to do with why I wasn't in class, and Ms. Triste waves me off. "Come in, you can just get started now."

Ms. Triste is familiar in a way that feels comfortable, not tense like sitting with Leila and James again. She keeps talking as I follow her toward the front of the room, moving her hands as if she's still painting.

The gestures remind me of my mother conducting her classical symphony. It's hard not to think of my mother when I'm in art class, but for once what I'm remembering isn't organizing her pills or getting her up in the morning. When I'm painting, it's easy for me to imagine how she feels when she's in her studio, humming and waving. And every trick I use—perspective, shading, light and dark—reminds me of sitting next to her while she taught me how to do it.

Ms. Triste gestures me into an empty chair. She waits beside the table as I arrange my backpack underneath the seat and pull out my sketchbook and a pencil. I'm not in my usual alphabetical-order seat because I joined the class late, so my view of the room, of Ms. Triste's paintings hanging on the walls, is a different one than I've had the last two years.

"The rules about quarterly projects haven't changed," Ms. Triste tells me. "The schedule of due dates is on the back bulletin board. You know what to do." She smiles again and moves off to another table, pinning her hair up with a pencil as she goes.

I open my sketchbook to the picture of my mother. I'll need something bigger for my final project this quarter, but Ms. Triste always tells us to start small. *You can make it bigger later, but you can't build on anything if you don't create something to start with.* And right now, this drawing of my mother in her white bed with a tray of wiggly foods over her lap is the only foundation I can think of. Maybe because she's all I seem to be able to think about.

I sketch intently, layering in clean and direct lines, as if now that I'm letting myself think about my mother, the world has snapped back into focus. I add the weave on the blanket and a pair of feet in old sneakers, just on the edge of the picture. My sneakers. The toes are pointed up, alert, but there's a hole in the canvas and one shoe's laces are untied. They droop onto the floor, waiting for someone to trip, like a prop in a melancholy oil painting.

I work steadily until the bell rings. This is the best part about having art last period: we never have to stop early to clean up.

As I cram my sketchbook and pencils into my bag, I notice that my deck of cards, the one I offered my mother, somehow ended up on the floor. I'm about to reach for it when someone bends down next to me and picks it up.

"Hey," says Natalie, holding the cards out, waiting while I put them away. The gesture surprises me. The other day, flopped on the grass talking about running away to the city, she didn't seem like the kind of person who would go out of her way to pick up something someone else had dropped.

"Are you going to your uncle's office today?"

I nod. Uncle John and I set up an official work schedule: Mondays, Thursdays, Saturdays.

"I'm driving over now if you want a ride," Natalie says. "I need to do some work with my pictures from Saturday."

"Sure," I say. I think I'm starting to crack the code of when Natalie's actually being friendly.

I follow her to her locker, standing on the other side of

the bright blue door while she shuffles books in and out of her bag, which is covered with patches and pins. When she stands up, somehow her bag is several inches thinner than mine, like all of her homework just evaporated into thin air. Following her through the hallways and out into the parking lot, watching her nod hello to some of the people we pass, I feel weighted down and uncool. As we pass Leila's usual spot, I turn my head away from it.

Natalie's car is gray and old, not silvery and new like Leila's. Through the back window, I can see stuff piled on the backseat: a few cardboard boxes, a dress on a hanger, a tripod, and a library book.

"You have to hit the door before you try to open it," Natalie tells me, pounding on her own door. "Three times, right next to the handle."

I do, banging the side of my fist against the gray metal. It feels oddly satisfying.

"I bargained with my mom for a car when my parents told my sister and me they were getting divorced," Natalie says as we climb in. "And then I bargained with my dad to teach me how to drive. It's not much of a car, but it gets me places."

I slide the seat back to create more room for my legs and my bag, which I'm nervous to toss on top of everything else in the backseat.

"I bet you ten dollars," Natalie says, "that when we get to the office, the first thing my mom will do is complain to you about the mess in my car."

I hear the annoyance in her voice, and I almost tell her then—that my mother is in the hospital; that when I talk to her, I'm not even sure she hears me. It's hard to get worked up about Natalie's mom thinking she doesn't keep her car clean enough.

So all I say is "I don't mind the mess."

That seems to be enough for Natalie, because she flicks the radio on and waves a hand at me to adjust the station.

Once we're out of the parking lot, Natalie lowers the volume, turns her head as much as she can while driving.

"So," she starts, "what's going on with you and that guy?"

I blink. "What guy?"

Then I realize she must mean James—she saw us the other day in the hall.

"Nothing," I say, but by the way Natalie scoffs, I'm guessing I said it a little too quickly or I'm blushing a little too much.

"Nothing," I say again, more emphatically. But I also start giggling for some reason, and so does she. "We're sort of friends?" I try. "We have English class together."

"Sure, that's all it is," she says, clearly not believing me at all. "I know your secret."

Hardly, I think. But as we sit there laughing and I keep shaking my head, I don't feel like I'm hiding anything.

———

Claire calls Natalie over as soon as we get there, looking stressed and impatient, and sits her at a computer, using the same big gestures Natalie does as she starts explaining something about the photos. Natalie looks at me and rolls her eyes, and I tilt my head back, my way of saying *I get it*. I do—but my stomach still hurts when I look at them together.

Natalie's mom is at least aware of her daughter's comings and goings. Natalie's mom is right here.

I watch them for only a moment before I cross the room to Uncle John's office, weaving between the desks and stepping carefully around the piles of paper that spill off tables onto the floor.

There are three other people leaning over Uncle John's table, and I don't want to interrupt their meeting. So I stand just outside the door, slightly off to one side, until he looks up and sees me. I'm tall enough to look over the visitors' heads, and I see drawings and photos spread out in front of them, heavy books holding down the corners.

"Sophie, come in, please," Uncle John says. He stands up, and the people in the chairs turn around.

I can tell just by looking that they're a family, a mother and father and daughter. The mother and daughter look

113

alike, more so than Natalie and Claire, with the same reddish-blond hair and identical noses and freckles. I have the urge to draw them, to try to capture the tiny similarities in their faces.

Uncle John smiles warmly at me. It's a smile I've seen him give other people over the last few days, but he hasn't directed it at me in years.

It surprises me, and I hope his clients don't notice that I hesitate before smiling back.

"Sophie, this is Trudy and Michael Carter and their daughter, Anne. Everyone, this is my niece, Sophie, who's one of our interns."

We all mumble hello, and Uncle John waves me into a chair and passes me a notepad and pencil. I take them and try to figure out what an actual intern who wanted to be here, who wanted to learn everything about architecture, would do with them.

"We just got started," Uncle John tells me. "The Carters own the plot of land we visited the other day." He points to the table, and when I look closely I see some of my sketches there. The photos are older, black and white. They must show what the house looked like before it became empty and rundown. The porch is level and the windows unbroken, and there's a gazebo in the backyard, a swing hanging from one of the trees.

"Sophie's just going to take some notes," Uncle John says, and I sit up straighter and perch my pencil over the pad. I listen to all the questions Uncle John asks about what the Carters need to change, what they would want to change if their budget were unlimited. I try to take down everything. For the first time in almost a week, I pay attention.

"We want to restore as much as possible," Trudy says, and I hope she means the gazebo and the swing too. "With one exception. My mother's going to be moving in with us, so we need to add some space on the first floor for her. She's in her seventies and she's been in and out of the hospital, and she's not moving so well anymore."

She stops. I look at my notepad and flip the page with a loud crinkle so I won't stare. *My mother's been in and out of the hospital*, Trudy said, and I wish I could ask her how she managed to say it so easily.

"I'm sorry to hear that." Uncle John's voice is steady, and he pauses until the Carters nod at him in acknowledgment. "We can definitely design the house, even with the restoration, to accommodate that." I remember to take notes again as he asks Trudy and Michael questions about how far Trudy's mom can walk and explains that they can add a ramp for her to the home's front stairs.

Finally Uncle John is done, and we all stand up at the same time and shake hands in a confusion of arms reaching over the desk. I wait in the office while Uncle John sees them out.

When he comes back in, I'm not expecting him to say, "So, are you ready?"

"Ready for what?"

"To help me with the project. The Carters' house." He sits back down, grabs a pad and starts sketching, explaining where he'll put windows to make the best use of the land's light and the way he'll create a separate bedroom-bathroom suite for Anne on the second floor.

"Now, what about this space for Trudy's mother on the first floor?"

He glances up at me. He's not just talking to himself. He's really asking.

I lean over the table, studying Uncle John's sketch. I think about the way I feel in Aunt Cynthia and Uncle John's house, never sure if I'm sitting in a chair one of them usually sits in or eating food that someone else was planning to have. Always out of place.

"Maybe you could add some rooms here, off the kitchen," I say, tracing my fingers over what he's drawn. He was pressing harder on the page than he had to for a sketch, and the lines are thick, the way I imagine braille. I wonder if Uncle John can read them, figure out the shapes of these people's lives, just by touch.

"She probably shouldn't have her own kitchen, in case she forgets to turn the stove off," I say. "But this way she can be right near it, so she won't have to walk through everyone else's space if she just wants to get a glass of water or something. And you're already expanding the second floor right above that spot to make the room for Anne."

I glance up at Uncle John and he's nodding and scribbling down notes, so I keep going. "Maybe she should have a bedroom and one other room, so she won't feel like she's being confined to a tiny corner of the house. And her own bathroom."

"Good," Uncle John says, sketching as I talk. "This is excellent, Sophie."

I think of Trudy's and Anne's faces, how I wanted to draw them. Now, by helping to design their house, I sort of am.

Except that Uncle John is doing the actual drawing. And as I watch him sketching out what I just said, the new bedroom and bathroom and small living room just off the kitchen, I realize something.

I say it before I really think about it: "I didn't know you could draw."

He looks up from the paper and smiles. "You didn't?"

"I know it's stupid," I say quickly. "Obviously, you're an architect. I guess I just never thought about it."

"We do most of the work on computer now, actually," he

says. "So I could probably get away with doing a lot less drawing. I just like to get my ideas down on paper first."

He leans forward and adds, "But I thought you knew that's how I met Cynthia—I took a drawing class with your mother, back when they were both living in New York."

He laughs a little, like a funny memory just popped into his head.

"No," I say. My throat is strangely dry and scratchy. "I didn't know that."

"Your mother threw a big party right after class ended, and she and Cynthia were sharing an apartment then. I went to the party with some friends, and Cynthia and I started talking and it was just..." he trails off, then shrugs and smiles, as if to say, *that was it.*

I know Aunt Cynthia and my mother used to share an apartment in New York, long before Leila and I were born. They told us so many stories about it—the bright walls covered with pictures my mother had painted, the way she designed a screen for a corner of the living room so Aunt Cynthia could wall it off into a study while she was in law school. Leila and I used to talk about doing the same thing when we got older, moving into the city together while Leila became a famous musician and I did whatever I decided I wanted to do. I imagined us in an apartment just like my mother and Aunt Cynthia's: small, but colorful and homey.

But I never thought about what their lives were actually like. I never imagined them throwing parties together, my mother introducing her sister to the quiet, nerdy-looking boy from art class.

Now I imagine Aunt Cynthia's life back then like a slide-show: eating dinner in a restaurant with the boy from the party; sitting in class, taking quick notes, ink stains on her hands; meeting friends on Friday night for a movie, maybe an independent film at an artsy theater downtown. I picture her raiding my mother's closet for something to wear when she goes out.

Uncle John clears his throat across from me and taps his pencil against the table. I look up, realizing I've been in a fog.

"Thanks for the help," he says. "I think this project is going to turn out well." He rolls up the floor plans, snapping a rubber band around them and setting them against a bookshelf.

"We should probably head home. Leila has jazz band on Mondays, so we usually eat early." He stands up, grabs his bag from a chair, and starts tossing things in—the notepad he's been using to sketch the Carters' new plans, a book, his cell phone, the smaller bag he uses to carry his lunch.

I almost open my mouth to stop him when he says the word home, remind him that where we're going isn't really my house. My home is the tiny apartment on the other side of town with two names on the mailbox, written in a younger me's capital letters across a peeling piece of tape: CANON, AMY AND SOPHIE.

But I don't know how to explain that, so all I do is follow Uncle John out of the office.

FOURTEEN

IN ENGLISH CLASS THE NEXT AFTERNOON, THE DESKS ARE
back in small clusters, and Mr. Jackson has us sit with our
groups from yesterday. James, Leila, and I settle silently into
our spots. Mr. Jackson looks at each group sternly as he tells
the class to quiet down. He doesn't have to look at us.

"This setup is just for a few minutes, so we can iron out
some details about the projects. Then we'll get back into the
usual rows," Mr. Jackson says. Leila's sigh of relief is so full
I think I actually feel her deflate next to me.

Mr. Jackson answers a few questions about the assignment and then passes out a sign-up sheet with presentation
dates. The first one is next week, and suddenly all I can think
is *I can't do this*. Actually sit with James and Leila in a room
and have a conversation and come up with posters or
costumes or *something* by then? No. But when the sheet gets

to us, that first slot has already been taken, and Leila writes our names in a messy scrawl, without asking us, next to the very last date.

"Do you really think…" James starts, as if he's about to disagree with the choice. But then he changes his mind, I guess, because he just shrugs and passes the sheet to the next group.

For once, I'm on Leila's side. Good, I think, as I watch her list our names at the bottom of the page. *Let's delay this thing as long as possible.*

———

James catches up to me after class, matching my pace as I head for the art room. It's at the far end of the hallway, so the crowd around us thins out quickly.

I wait for James to turn off into a classroom or say something, but he doesn't do either. So finally, just outside art, I stop and face him.

"What?" I snap.

"What do you mean?" His rumbly voice answers.

I roll my eyes. "I *mean*," I say, standing straighter and channeling Leila as best I can, "why are you following me?"

James shrugs, his backpack bouncing up and down on his shoulders. "I'm walking to band. You're walking to art. It's in the same direction."

I give up. I reach for the doorknob and start to turn it

before James says, "Wait." When I look back at him over my shoulder, his hand is stretched toward my arm. He pulls it back.

"I just...you looked kind of out of it in English the other day. And then today you seemed upset. Are you sure you're okay?"

He looks at me steadily, as if he can draw the answer telepathically out of my brain, and all I can do is blink at him. My mind is completely empty. No answer to offer, telepathic or otherwise. And then we're just looking at each other, and I forget I'm even supposed to be thinking of one.

The second bell rings and we both jump.

James finally looks down. "See you in English, I guess," he says, and I still haven't said anything by the time he turns around and walks away.

———

In the classroom I grab an easel from the cluster at the back of the room and set it up next to my seat. I rapidly paint thick black lines on the page, in no pattern whatsoever. I'm not trying to paint anything in particular. I'm just trying not to think about James watching me and then following me through the hall. Why is he suddenly so intent on talking to me? He didn't really answer my question, and part of me wants to chase after him and ask again. What, what, *what?*

After a few minutes, I stop the frantic movement of my

paintbrush and stare at what I've done, tilting my head. My body is still buzzing, so I close my eyes and force myself to think only about what I can make out of this random jumble of lines. When something comes, I move my brush toward the page and begin to paint.

Which is when Natalie appears next to my table, photos in hand, on her way to talk to Ms. Triste.

"Hey," she says, stopping in front of my easel. She looks at the lines, crinkling her forehead. After a moment she nods, not saying anything about what a giant mess the painting is right now. I appreciate it.

"Listen," she says. "My boyfriend is going to be here after school. Can you come out with us? I could use your help with something."

Me? Even though we've been hanging out the past few days, my first impulse is still to ask Natalie why. Why me when she could ask one of her other friends, when her boyfriend is coming all the way here from the city?

But I catch myself before I ask her. Because I do want to go out with them, to do pretty much anything that isn't sitting in Aunt Cynthia's guest room, pretending to do my homework while I wait for visiting hours at the hospital.

When I look over, Natalie is still staring at my easel, her head tilted to the right. She doesn't look at me, but when I say okay, she smiles, and her fingers squeeze the top corner of my easel as she leaves.

———

This time I stand on the other side of Natalie's locker door, looking at the photos and postcards and notes. There's a theme to the way she decorated her locker, black and white postcards of bridges and beaches, and sepia-toned photos of women in long, cumbersome dresses. I'll have to ask Uncle John to show her the old photos of the Carters' house.

My eyes find one spot of color in the corner, a photo of Natalie with Claire and a tall man who I decide must be her father. He and Claire are standing on either side of Natalie, arms around her shoulders, all three of them smiling and wearing dressy clothes. A younger girl, who must be Natalie's sister, stands on their father's other side, wearing a velvet dress with a bow. But the photo is tucked away behind a postcard, as if Natalie wasn't quite sure what to do with it.

The photo in the center of the locker is black and white, not color, but I recognize Natalie in it. She's sitting on a bed, behind a tall, thin boy in a button-down shirt. She has one arm around his neck, and his head is turned slightly behind him, like he's about to talk to her. I know without asking that he must be her boyfriend, but he doesn't look the way I imagined. No headphones or weird T-shirt.

Natalie shuts the locker and stands up, and I'm staring at air where the pictures were. Natalie's bag looks nearly empty again, but she took her camera out of her locker, and she holds it against her body with one arm.

"Ready?" she asks.

We walk together down the hall, past clusters of other people packing up for the day. We're nearly at the door when Natalie says, "Hey, isn't that—"

I look up. James is standing there.

And he's talking to Leila and a girl with white-blond hair who I assume must be Leila's friend Liz, the one she promised to drive home.

I resist the urge to stomp my foot. Somehow, Leila and James always manage to be where I least want to run into them. And then I have to ignore the swooping thing that happens in my stomach whenever I look over to where James is standing.

I'm trying to think of something to say to Natalie—to remind her that nothing is going on—when I realize she's already walking across the hall, straight to James. Leila and Liz have already turned away, but James sees me before I can get Natalie's attention.

"Hey, Sophie," he says. I stop walking. I realize after a minute of awkward silence that Natalie's stopped too and that I guess I should introduce them.

126

"Um," I start. "This is Natalie." I wave a hand at her. "Natalie, this is James."

I don't know whether to use the words *my friend* for either of them, so I leave them out.

"We were just going…" and I trail off, realizing I have no idea where we're going. I'm leaning toward the door, trying to communicate to Natalie how urgently I want to go, but she's not taking the hint.

"Actually," she says, looking at James, "are you doing anything right now? We could use one more person." She's totally direct, like this is a normal thing to ask a complete stranger.

I stare at her. What is she doing? I don't even know why she needs my help, let alone the help of a third person she's never even met.

But James gives me a quick look and agrees, and soon he and I are following Natalie out to her car. We're waiting, next to each other and not talking, while Natalie moves her boxes and hanger and tripod out of the backseat. We're climbing in, me in the front seat, which I've pulled up slightly for James's long legs, and James in the back. Then we're lining up behind the other cars for the crawl out of the parking lot, James asking Natalie about how we know each other and what classes she's taking. At first, Natalie hardly answers, but the more questions James asks, the more animated she gets, the same way she did when I asked about her photos. I stay quiet, but I listen, feeling hyper-aware of everything.

———

I had no idea where Natalie was taking us, and I especially wasn't expecting the Carters' plot of land, the rundown house. The building looks the same, droopy and mysterious, but for now the tall table in front of it is empty. There's no one around, from Uncle John's office or otherwise.

James unfolds himself from the backseat, but Natalie waits a moment before turning off the car, so I stay where I am too. She leans over the gearshift and nudges her chin in James's direction.

"Just go for it," she says. "Seriously."

"I don't—" I start to protest, but Natalie just looks at me and shakes her head, like I shouldn't even bother trying to pretend I don't think James is cute. It's the kind of conversation I was imagining this morning, a version of the conversations eleven-year-old Leila and I used to have.

I follow Natalie around to the back of the car. There's an even more random sampling of things in her trunk than in her backseat. I spot a few cans of paint, a single boot, and at least five cardboard boxes.

She hands two of them to James and me and nods toward the house. Whatever's inside rattles and clanks as we carry the cartons.

"Chain mail?" James guesses.

"Tambourines?" I suggest. We shake our boxes in unison, and James does a silly jumping dance move with his. I laugh.

We keep thinking of possible items in Natalie's boxes until we get back to where Natalie's standing with the boy I saw in her locker photo, who's holding the handlebars of his bicycle. He leans down to kiss her, and I look away, but not before I see how comfortable they are together.

"This is Zach," Natalie says, and we all start talking over ourselves as we introduce one another.

We take the last of the boxes from the trunk and Natalie, now with her camera around her neck, leads the way to the house again. But instead of stopping at the doorway, where James and I left the other two boxes, she steps up onto the rickety porch. She takes another step and another, and then she's inside the house. The wood dips and creaks in the places she's walked.

"Are you sure we should go in there?" I call. "It doesn't seem totally stable." *And Uncle John and Claire would never want us to be in here.*

"Don't worry," Natalie shouts back from somewhere in the house. "It's fine in here."

And I realize she must have gone inside before, maybe the other day after I left.

No one else objects, so I follow James and Zach into the

house, shushing the mental voice that tells me this is the kind of thing my mother would do.

Natalie's right, mostly. There are some broken beams and piles of shattered window glass, but as we tiptoe in, the floor stays solid under us.

Natalie tells us how she wants it all set up, and we move through the house, still testing the floorboards in each new room. I end up in the living room with Zach, unfolding a rug and laying out a toy train track while he sets out a photo in a frame and tapes a curtain-like piece of cream-colored fabric to the window frame. The fake curtain flutters when a breeze blows through the broken window, and the effect is spooky.

As we work, Zach tells me how he and Natalie met: at a summer arts program, where he was writing and she was taking photos.

"He asked me to illustrate one of his stories," Natalie says, walking into the room. "I didn't realize no one else had their stories illustrated, and it was just a ploy to hang out."

Zach laughs. "You did fall for it."

James, standing in the doorway behind Natalie, looks at me over the top of her head, a faint smile on his face, and my stomach goes weird again, like I lost a breath between my nose and my lungs. I wonder if Natalie said anything to him about our conversation in the car.

Before I can come up with something, anything, to say, Natalie starts directing us around the room. We stand just on the other side of the doorway while she snaps pictures of the props. Then she adds us to the scene: Zach in the kitchen, holding a frying pan and spatula over the rusted stove; James and me in the living room, driving the wooden train around the track on the rug. I feel eight years old again as we crouch there, attaching the train cars with magnets.

"This feels like what we used to do when we were little," James says.

"That's what I was thinking," I tell him. Natalie's camera clicks just as I look up at him. I want to grab it and look at the picture so I can know the expression on my own face.

"If Leila were here, she would have made up a whole story about what the trains are doing," James adds.

"And told us exactly how we should be moving them around," I finish. We smile ruefully at each other, and again I feel like James is on my side, two against one.

"Keep talking!" Natalie calls to us as she moves around the room, getting each of us from every possible angle. She seems happier here, and I think of how good her photos of the house were once she remembered that she cared. Right now she's totally focused on how she wants this to work.

And somehow James and I do keep talking, as he tells me

about the band that he and Leila are in with some friends and the songs they're prepping for a battle of the bands next month, about the summer he spent working at his mom and Aunt Cynthia's law office.

I try to ask questions and say *mhmm* at normal points in the conversation. I don't say anything about my mother, about why I'm living at Leila's house now, about how I spent my summer, about working at Uncle John's office. I just hope James listens to what I am saying and doesn't notice what I'm not.

Finally Natalie finishes her photo shoot, and as we pack everything back into the boxes, she explains to us what the whole thing was about.

"I have some photos in a show at the arts center next month," she says. "But I wasn't happy with them anymore. It didn't seem like they represented any of the things I was trying to say. So I decided to put together some new work to show."

She clears her throat and looks around at the house. "I was thinking about what home means, and what happens when people's homes shift around them."

I think of all the versions of this house I've already seen, in the old photos and my sketch and Natalie's two sets of pictures.

"Anyway, this is what I came up with." She sort of shrugs, not looking at any of us.

"It's really cool," Zach says, and I can tell from his expression—which I wish Natalie would look up to see—just how much he means it.

———

Natalie drops Zach off at the train first.

"I'll talk to you later," Natalie says softly to him as he gets out of the car. She seems gentler around him, less on edge, and I smile, watching them from the backseat. Then I blush, remembering that James is watching them too.

Zach grabs his bike from the trunk and then leans in to say good-bye to us through the back windows. When he tells me how nice it was to meet me, I say it back automatically, politely, before I realize I genuinely mean it.

I expect James to move to the front so he can stretch his legs. But instead he stays in the back next to me, his arm resting along the top of the seat. I think again of all the things I haven't said to him, about everything that's going on with me, and then I tell my brain to stop. Instead I let myself be aware of his arm on the seat, the way he's leaning just slightly toward me, until we get to his house. It feels nice.

And then it's just Natalie and me in the car, and rather than asking me for directions to Uncle John and Aunt Cynthia's house, she asks, "Do you need to go home yet?"

"No." I don't think anyone there really keeps track of where I am.

133

"Good," Natalie says, turning into town. "Do you want to come over?"

She waits for a light and then turns again, into the parking lot of the pharmacy. "I just need to pick something up first."

"Okay." I follow her out of the car, taking my wallet, even though there's barely any money in it.

Natalie heads for the hair products aisle and crouches down, searching for something on the lowest shelf. When she stands up, she's holding two boxes of dye, one the same bright blue she has in her hair and another of neon pink.

"For my sister," she says, waving the pink box. Then she looks at me, tilting her head like she's setting up a photograph without her camera. She reaches down again, pulling a box of purple dye off the shelf.

"This one would work for you," she says. She turns it toward me. "What do you think?"

I study the photo. The color is dark, less noticeable than the blue or the pink. But it would be obvious in bright light, bold and new.

I hold out my hand for the box.

But the line at the front of the store is long, and the wait feels even longer after a woman with a crying baby and a full basket reaches the counter, slowing everything up.

Natalie turns toward the back of the store. "Let's try the pharmacy counter instead."

134

So we march back through the aisles to the pharmacy, where there are only four people ahead of us in line.

Three people.

Two people.

One person.

And then, when the man at the counter leans over to sign his receipt, I see the pharmacist who's working today, and I realize I know him. He's been giving me my mother's prescriptions every Friday for two years.

I'm frozen, staring at him, wondering how I could have forgotten that this is the pharmacy where I always pick up my mother's pills. Then I try to shift behind Natalie, so he can help her first and she won't hear the pharmacist ask about my mother. But he sees me before I can move.

"I have your prescription," he says. "Last week's too. I'll be right back."

He turns into the shelves and I turn too, hoping there's someone behind me I could pretend he was talking to. But Natalie and I are the only ones left in the line, and I can tell Natalie's looking at me, probably wanting to know more.

I think fast, wondering if I can explain why the pharmacist recognizes me and what prescription he's talking about without actually telling her anything. But I don't see a way.

I set my box of purple hair dye down on the counter.

"I have to go," I tell Natalie, still not looking at her.

And then I walk as quickly as I can out of the store. I hit Natalie's car door three times, right next to the handle, and pull my backpack from the floor of the front seat. Then I pull my bag on and walk back the way we drove, through town and past the train station and toward Leila's house, even though no one is waiting for me.

FIFTEEN

I'M GLAD MY LOCKER IS A FEW HALLWAYS AWAY FROM Natalie's, because the next day, when I slide down in front of it to eat my lunch, I don't have to worry that she'll walk by when I don't want to see her.

When I got back to Aunt Cynthia and Uncle John's house last night, hurrying up the stairs to avoid everyone, I found a message on my phone from Dr. Choi's office, asking me to meet with him this afternoon. *This is a message for Sophie Canon. Dr. Choi would like to discuss Amy's treatment plan.* Another reminder that I had stopped thinking about her for one afternoon.

Now, once again, she fills my thoughts despite all my attempts to distract myself. I try to sink into the familiar rhythms of my lunch period, tuning out the sounds of lockers slamming on either side of me. I chew my sandwich absentmindedly as I fly through the equations I was supposed to balance for chemistry class today. I have half an hour to get through them all and review my notes in case there's a pop quiz.

But when I finish the problem set and look back over my work, I don't even need my calculator to see the page is covered with careless errors, reactants I forgot to multiply and elements I didn't balance. For once, I give up on the assignment before lunch ends. I slam the book shut, leaving the sheet of messy equations inside, now with a crease probably slanted across the page. I stare at the floor, suddenly noticing how many of the feet that pass me are in clusters while I sit here by myself.

And when I open my locker, looking for something else to do, all I can see is the inside of the door, empty of photos or postcards or reminder notes or even one of those small magnetic mirrors. If I hadn't just used my own combination on the lock, I would have no idea the few books piled inside belong to me at all.

After lunch, after chemistry—where I guess my way through the pop quiz—after gym and English, skipping art is easy. Easier than trying to tell Natalie why I rushed out of the pharmacy and had gone by the time she came outside. Why I can't stay after school to work on our art projects. Easier than telling her the way my stomach hurts when I think about the conversation I have to have with Dr. Choi this afternoon. And much easier than explaining to Natalie who Dr. Choi is in the first place. I could make up a story, but when I try to think of something, my mind stays empty.

So as everyone else scurries to eighth period, I hurry down the hall, head down, and push through the exit, listening for the now-familiar ka-thunk as the door locks behind me. James hasn't followed me down the hall this time, and I ignore the part of me that wishes he had. Outside, my legs don't need me to tell them which way to walk. They just go, powered by muscle memory. My mind has other things to worry about, like what my mother's doctor has to tell me.

———

"Sophie Canon?"

The nurse calls my name from the doorway to the doctors' offices too soon after I sit down. Even though skipping art got me here early and I've been waiting a while, I'm not ready to go in yet. I stand up and cross the waiting room slowly, keeping my eyes on the floor. I wonder whether anyone—or everyone—around me thinks I'm a patient. Whether there's any way to tell, just by looking, which of the people here are healthy and which aren't. I see no obvious clues.

Dr. Choi, sitting behind a wide cherrywood desk, stands up to shake my hand when the nurse shows me in.

"Sophie, it's good to see you again. Please have a seat."

I sit. My backpack looks scruffy against Dr. Choi's dark carpet and wooden furniture, and I shove it under my chair with one foot. Then I rearrange myself so I'm sitting on my hands, to keep myself from twisting my fingers together while Dr. Choi is talking. I look up at him. *Okay.* I breathe. *Here it comes.*

Dr. Choi sits down again, across from me, and rests his hands on the desk, his fingers knit neatly together. He has perfect posture, and again he reminds me of a water bird.

"I have some good news," Dr. Choi says. "Your mother has stabilized enough for us to evaluate her, and she seems to be responding well to the Depakote, the medication we put her on when she was first admitted. It tends to be effective for patients dealing with mixed states. We're working on finding the minimum possible dosage, but it will take three or four weeks until we have an exact sense of how well the treatment is working."

Three or four weeks? I remember Dr. Choi telling me very clearly that it would be ten days, the same amount of time I told Aunt Cynthia and Uncle John. The room tilts and panic rushes in. *What went wrong?* And then, *will it be like this for another three weeks?*

I grip the edges of my seat tightly, waiting, saying nothing. Dr. Choi has done this before; he must know all the things I want to say. All the questions I want to ask.

He glances down at my mother's chart, open on his desk, then back at me. The chart is slanted away from me, so all I can tell is that it's covered in dark, neat handwriting, my mother's entire messy, up-and-down past reduced to a few orderly cursive lines.

"Your mother's medical history shows she's bounced back and forth among a lot of different therapists," Dr. Choi says. "She needs more consistent care to manage her illness, and having a social worker didn't seem to be enough monitoring last time. I'd like to send her to an outpatient treatment facility once she's released from the hospital. She could attend group therapy sessions there, but she would also be able to start reestablishing her own routines at home."

He pauses, picks up a pen, jots something down on a pad on his desk.

In the silence, I let Dr. Choi's words wash over me, and I can feel my head moving in a nod of understanding. But I don't think I actually heard him. Even though I'm trying to listen, everything he's saying seems to be traveling to me from some other planet. As if I won't hear it for light-years, and by the time it reaches me, Dr. Choi's face will be gray and wrinkled on the other side of the desk. I think I've regressed back into the foggy-headed state I've been in since the afternoon I found my mother.

But then a few of his words reach out and grab me, pull me back: *outpatient facility; reestablishing her routines at home.*

"So you're going to be able to send her home soon?" I ask.

But there's something weird about my voice. It doesn't sound excited. It sounds anxious and maybe a little bit frightened. And I can't see my face, but my mouth feels frozen in something that isn't quite a smile.

Dr. Choi's own calm expression turns downward slightly, just for a second. "I do still think she should be stable enough to leave after she's been here about two weeks, yes," he says.

There's an unspoken *but* at the end of his sentence.

"She's done fairly well up to this point," Dr. Choi finally continues. "Her situation doesn't seem severe enough to merit sending her to an inpatient facility, and I know we're dealing with a limited health insurance plan that won't cover most inpatient treatments. But she will need monitoring to make sure she keeps up with her medications and out-patient therapy."

Dr. Choi is leading up to something. I keep my hands on the sides of my chair, holding tightly.

"It looks like you've essentially been your mother's caregiver for a few years now, Sophie," Dr. Choi says.

A little more than five years, I think. But again I say nothing.

"It's a lot to ask for you to monitor your mother's medication and care. I'm sure you also have schoolwork and other responsibilities. So I hope you'll consider other options for getting your mother help. We can recommend some resources in the community, or maybe there's a neighbor or a relative who could assist you."

I want to laugh. A loud, wild, that's-not-actually-funny laugh, a booming *ha ha ha*. I wonder what Dr. Choi would do if I did.

I think about my options—asking Aunt Cynthia and Uncle John for help, probably offering to take more hours at Uncle John's office; trying to find a neighbor in our crowded, loud apartment building who isn't too busy with her own job and life to watch my mother every day. I think about how hard turning our upside-down life right-side-up would be.

Laughing seems like the only possible response.

"Here's the information about the outpatient facility," Dr. Choi says. He tears the top sheet from his notepad and passes it to me. I look down and see a name, address, and phone number, but my eyes don't actually read them.

I stand up slowly and put out my hand, the one that isn't clutching the paper, to shake Dr. Choi's. I hope I look steady and sure, put-together like the polished office I'm standing in.

"Thanks," I tell him. We trade nods and slight smiles. "I'm sure I can figure something out."

It's not until I'm in the hall, moving slowly back toward the waiting room, that I realize my arms and legs are shaking.

I don't know what the doctors have told my mother about her treatment, so I walk toward her room, wobbly legs and all, to share what I heard from Dr. Choi. I plan out what I'm going to say, complete with upbeat tone and perky smile.

Great news, Mom! I spoke to your doctor and they're going to be able to send you home soon. You'll just have to go to regular therapy sessions at an outpatient treatment center. It's not far from here, and you can be at home and start painting again. It'll be better than being here, I promise.

As I walk down the hall, it feels like there are two of me. One version is imagining what my mother will say when I tell her the news. The other is wondering why I'm not hurrying to her room faster. Why there's a small part of me hoping maybe she won't be awake when I get there.

But she is.

She's staring at the TV, watching a nature program. On the screen, a brown bear leads a train of cubs through the woods as the deep documentary narrator voice explains the

144

relationship between mother bears and their offspring. How bears will mostly leave people alone unless we're dumb enough to get between a mother and a cub.

"Hi, Mom," I say, the same way I always do. I reach for the remote on the rolling tray and turn down the volume until I'm sure she'll be able to hear me. She turns her head to look at me and says hello back. Does her voice sound better, more animated, today? I tell myself it does.

Instead of taking my usual chair, I perch on the edge of the bed near her feet. I'm not shaking anymore, but I still feel jittery, like I've had too much caffeine or sugar. I reach out to touch one of her feet, solid under the blanket, to anchor myself here.

A memory flashes through my mind of her playing five little piggies with my toes after a bath. It feels like something that happened a very long time ago, maybe to someone who wasn't even me.

"I just came from talking to Dr. Choi," I tell her. "Your doctor here," I add in case she doesn't remember. "He thinks they'll be able to discharge you soon, maybe in a week. Then we can get you home again." *And this little piggy ran all the way home.*

My words fall into the space between my mother and me. They sound curiously flat, not upbeat or perky, even though I'm following my script.

"That's good," my mother says. But her voice sounds listless too, just the way it has for the past few days, not better like I imagined. She doesn't say anything else.

Sitting there, watching her, I feel my face heat up and the corners of my eyes start to burn. I think of those mornings when I pretended to be a waiter, offering her breakfast, cajoling her out of bed, bringing in her plate of pills, and the way she would lie there, hardly responding.

Why won't anything I say ever get her to *talk*?

I wonder what James and Natalie and Zach and Leila are doing right now. Certainly not this.

Why is everything about our life the reverse of everyone else's?

I take my hand away from her foot and knot it together with my other hand in my lap. It doesn't matter that our life is different. Right now, here, I have a job. I'm the calm one, the one who doesn't swing from one extreme to another when the seasons change or I stop taking my medications or I haven't had enough sleep.

"How are you feeling today, Mom?" I ask. "Is your head any better, or still fuzzy?"

She mumbles her answer, and I have to lean closer to hear. "It's a little better," she says, her lips hardly moving.

"That's good," I reply.

I try to sound bright, as if, in my script, there's an exclamation point at the end of this line. But again there's something off about how it comes out.

My usual routine of acting cheerful until my mother starts to do the same isn't working.

I study the empty air between us, as if I'll be able to see the invisible wires that keep energy flowing from me to her and back again. If I find them, maybe I can press the call button by my mother's bed and bring in a doctor to fix the one that's broken.

We sit in silence on the bed. I pick at the blanket, the same way I do in Aunt Cynthia's guest room, and listen to the sounds of the hospital: the rolling food carts and IV poles, the beeps of patients' machines down the hall, the careful modulations of a doctor's voice as she tells a patient how he's doing.

I'm still leaning toward my mother. My body seems sure she's about to say something. But my head knows otherwise. My mother's eyes are back on the TV screen, watching the line of cubs follow their mother through the woods. The mother bear doesn't turn around as the cubs and the camera track her. She just lumbers between the trees, confident the others are behind her.

I realize what I'm waiting for my mother to say: the kinds of things mothers usually say to their daughters when they get home from school every afternoon, maybe while they're sitting together at the kitchen table with a snack, legs swinging under their chairs, flicking through the day's mail.

"How are you today, Sophie?" I ask in my closest imitation of my mother's voice. The question cuts across the mix of beeps and far-off doctors' murmurs and bear sounds from the TV.

My mother's head shifts back toward me on her pillow. She looks confused. A small part of me feels guilty for adding to what must already be a muddle in her head.

But right now, the part of me that wants to keep talking is louder.

My voice gets higher and more sarcastic until it's not actually a good impression of my mother at all. "How was your day at school, honey? Learn anything interesting? What did you have for lunch?"

Shut up, the voice in the back of my head says, taking her side. *You know it's not her fault she's like this.*

My mother is still looking at me, staring straight into my face, not talking. I look right back, at her concave cheeks and uneven hair and long fingers that usually spend their days conducting imaginary classical symphonies and swirling colors on a canvas, not resting on hospital blankets. The fingers that paint away for hours while I sit on the floor of her studio and narrate my day to her, whether or not she's listening.

This is just how she is sometimes, the voice reminds me.

I ignore it.

"I ate lunch in the hallway by myself again today," I tell my mother. The words come out evenly, even though calm is the last thing I feel. "I'm working in Uncle John's office after school and on weekends so that he and Aunt Cynthia will help out with your hospital bills. I'm living in their guest room. You used to stay there, I'm sure you remember. Until—"

I stop. My mind flashes back to the summer before sixth grade, the last time we stayed together at Aunt Cynthia and Uncle John's house. Before Leila stopped returning my calls and Aunt Cynthia stopped coming over to cook with my mother in our tiny kitchen or go shopping with her at the mall. I realize I don't actually know what to say next. Until *what?*

"Leila drives me to school every day, but we spend most of the time not talking to each other, and I've hardly seen Aunt Cynthia since last week."

Now, finally, I sound the way I feel, my voice clogged and uneven like I'm crying. But when I reach up to touch my face, there's no water there. The tears are still waiting at the corners of my eyes while the furious words in my head try to fit themselves together into sentences.

There's a whole other part to how I am that I don't say a word about: talking to Natalie at work, my afternoon with her and Zach and James at the house, pretending to be other people. The part of my life that's been better since my mother left.

The part that will have to disappear as soon as she comes home.

I stand up.

I mumble a good-bye, not letting myself look back at the familiar face on the pillow, and leave the room. I move so slowly down the hall I probably look like one of the patients who shuffle along beside me, the bottoms of their hospital gowns flapping around their knees.

It's not until I'm in the elevator, punching the button for the lobby again and again and again and please nobody else get on and why won't the doors shut already and then finally they do, that I let myself think the rest of my thought.

Maybe I don't want my mother to come home.

SIXTEEN

I WAKE UP IN THE GUEST ROOM BED, UNDER THE COVERS in all my clothes, to the sound of the doorbell ringing.

My eyes feel dry and itchy and my legs are twisted in the sheets, as if I was trying to run away from something in a dream. But I don't remember what I was dreaming about. I don't even remember falling asleep.

When I roll over, I see one red sneaker on the floor next to the bed, the untied lace trailing across the hole that's frayed open near the toe. The other shoe is next to the desk. I vaguely remember kicking it off and hearing it bounce against the wood before I burrowed into the blankets.

My stomach growls and I check the clock: 7:53. But is it a.m. or p.m.?

The bell rings again and someone opens the front door

below me. I put my ear to the wall to listen. Aunt Cynthia calls for Leila, who clomps down the stairs to my left and starts talking to whoever's at the door. A low voice answers her, and I hear it say my name.

I sit up fast. It's definitely p.m.

That's James's voice in the front hall; I completely forgot about the meeting for our English project. I shove my feet into my shoes, not bothering to tie them, and dash into the bathroom to throw water on my face.

In the mirror, my eyes are red-edged and wisps of hair stick straight out from the sides of my head. I look like I spent the whole afternoon brushing my hair with a balloon. I study my own face and think of one of the words from that list I made in the lunchroom on the first day of sixth grade, after Kelly whirled her finger around her ear to tell her friend who I was, the crazy woman's daughter: I look *deranged*. If one of the nurses from the hospital saw me right now, they wouldn't need to ask whether I'm related to my mother.

Don't start that right now.

The warning voice in the back of my head won't even let me think about what *that* is. Won't let me remember any of the things I said or thought this afternoon.

I pat my face dry and run my fingers through my hair. I step into the hall without another glance at the mirror.

Focus. English project. Downstairs.

———

"Pizza?"

James holds a slice out to me on a paper plate that's already spotted with grease. He showed up with two boxes of pizza still in one of those red vinyl cases pizza delivery guys carry, and I realized that when James said he'd come over after work, he must have meant work at the pizza place downtown.

I look up from where I'm staring at the hole in my shoe, and James peers into my face. "Are you—"

"Thanks." I cut him off and grab the plate out of his hand. I don't even want to let him ask whatever he's wondering about, whether I'm okay or if I've been crying or if I've ever owned a hairbrush. I remember the feeling of sitting next to him in Natalie's car yesterday and very carefully don't look at him again.

I'm sure he'll give up if I don't answer.

I wait, tense, watching Leila blot at her pizza with napkins to sop up the grease, until James picks up his own slice and bites into it. Now I can eat; I know question time is over.

We're sitting on the floor of Leila's room, poetry anthologies and pens and notebooks spread out in front of us. I haven't been in this room since we were eleven, but it looks almost exactly the way it did then, the same gray carpet and deep purple quilt and wide white desk. The same lampshade we decorated with glitter and shapes cut out of pink and purple construction paper.

The same painting on the wall over the bed, right where Leila can see it from her desk, of two little girls in shorts and T-shirts, one wearing orange and the other pink, sitting back-to-back on a wide rock. They're smiling at the painter.

My mother took forever to get the painting right, because Leila and I kept trying to make each other laugh. The rock got hotter and hotter in the sun, and we hated sitting still on it. But that's part of what makes the painting work. We both look like we're almost in motion, all our energy ready for the moment when we're free to leap up and go play.

"All right, let's do this," Leila suddenly says next to me, pretending to sound tough.

I look around. In the time I've been staring at the painting, she's finished her pizza, and James is on his second slice, or maybe his third. If this were yesterday, I might have teased him about it or made a comment to Natalie and Zach. But now it doesn't feel right.

I have to stop thinking about what Natalie and Zach would do, because soon my mother will be home and it won't matter. I won't be able to hang out with them anymore.

Leila opens the anthology and runs her finger down the

table of contents. I chew my pizza slowly to the sound of the book's thin pages flipping.

"Stop me when I get to a poet you like," Leila tells us.

She reads down the list of names. She pauses at a few that sound familiar, reads the first three or four lines of each poem, moves on. Once, James asks her to stop, but he shakes his head after only a few lines.

"Nah," he says. "Too sappy. No romantic poems."

See! I would tell Natalie if she were here. *No romantic poems, so it's not what you're thinking.*

I ignore the flash of disappointment in my stomach at that thought.

I finish my pizza and lie down on Leila's floor, empty paper plate on my stomach. I can't focus on anything Leila is reading. The words that drift over to me, about love and nightmares and rainstorms, are so much less real than any of the thoughts already filling my head. Those thoughts take turns parading across my mind like lines in a chorus. My mother, Dr. Choi, Natalie and Zach, the mother bear and her cubs on TV. Leila and my mother and me in the car. Aunt Cynthia, passing us department store bags with matching sundresses inside; Uncle John ruffling Leila's hair. The sixth grade lunchroom, Leila's and James's tables already noisy and full, nobody offering me a space. James, following me down the hall.

My stomach hurts. I put my hand over it and hear a crinkling sound. Now my palm is on top of the greasy paper plate I already forgot was there. Yuck.

"Sophie?" I turn my head toward James's voice. He and Leila are both looking at me. Leila keeps turning her mouth down, as if she's trying not to laugh.

"What do you think about that one? It's the only one we both like so far," James says. He's looking curious again, the way he did when I first walked into the room.

"I don't know," I answer, because I wasn't listening to Leila read at all. I realize my hand is still on the plate and I shift, sending it sliding to the floor. It leaves tomato sauce and stringy melted cheese on my fingers. Gross.

Leila's shoulders quiver.

And apparently that's all it takes, because suddenly that angry-terrified feeling I had in the hospital elevator comes right back.

I sit up. When I put my hands on the floor to lean on, one of them lands on the pizza plate again. My cousin giggles.

I don't think it's funny.

I glare at her and fling the plate away from my hand, hard, like a Frisbee. Leila stops giggling.

"Does it really matter what I think?" I ask. My voice is even but my insides aren't; they're shaking again, like there's

156

a miniature person in my stomach jumping up and down on a trampoline. Neither Leila nor James answers me.

"I mean it," I say. I glance at James, but really, I'm talking to Leila. "I wasn't even in your group until Mr. Jackson put me there, and you weren't happy about it. Do you really care what I think about the stupid project?"

Now they're both staring at me.

Leila looks surprised, her eyes wide and her mouth hanging slightly open in a way that would make Uncle John tease her about catching flies. James is just watching, taking in everything that happens, not intervening between my cousin and me. The way he did in sixth grade when I stood behind the lunch table, waiting for someone to talk to me. A part of me wants to shout at him too.

Just say something, James.

Then, to my surprise, he does.

"Leila—" he starts in a tone that makes me think he's actually about to take my side.

But the words are building up in my throat and, actually, I *don't* want James to speak.

I want to speak.

I look at Leila. I'm glaring again, trying to ignore the stringy pizza cheese on my fingers.

"It doesn't seem like you care what I think," I tell her. My voice is louder now. I want to add *when you blast your music* and ignore me in the car. *When you spend as much time out of the house as you possibly can. When you haven't asked about my mother since that first morning after I got here.* I don't say those things. I'm afraid of what will happen, of what I'll say next, once I let myself start.

All I say is "It seems like you haven't cared much about what's going on with me for—oh—the last five years."

"Sophie, that's not—" Leila finally tries to say something.

But I turn away from her and she stops. I stand up and retrieve my plate, crumple it in one hand, and toss it at Leila's trashcan. As it lands with a thunk against the metal, solid and satisfying, I step over the pizza box and James's backpack. I leave my book where it is on the floor. From the doorway, I look back at my cousin and say the last thing I need to let out.

"So why start caring now?"

SEVENTEEN

I GET UP EARLY THE NEXT MORNING AND LEAVE FOR school before Leila even comes downstairs. All through the long walk on our town's quiet early morning sidewalks, then in the empty school hallways, I feel hollow, like someone's used an ice cream scoop to remove my insides. There's no more trampoline in my stomach, and only the dull echo of that chorus of thoughts in my head. I'm distantly amazed that my body is still walking to class, still opening and closing my locker, still changing into my gym clothes the way it does on any other day.

In second period math class, I've become the person Mr. Borakov calls on when no one else can figure out an answer to one of his questions. Usually I have the equation solved already, the answer scribbled in my notes.

But today when he scans the class, sees no hands up, and

says, "Sophie?" I look at my notebook and realize I haven't even written down the problem. I shake my head and look down at my desk. When the bell rings, I dash out of the room.

———

I know I can't skip art again without a better excuse for Ms. Triste, but after English, where Mr. Jackson tries to coach us through analyzing a poem, I walk to eighth period as slowly as I can, taking a detour through the science hallway in case James tries to catch up with me.

I get to the art room just after the bell rings, and I grab an easel, looking anywhere but at Natalie's seat as I set the easel up next to my chair. I'm working with watercolors, but I know within three minutes that I'm not painting well. I'm too tense and stiff, my feet stuck to one spot on the floor and my hand jabbing at the paper.

"Hey," Natalie's voice comes from somewhere near me.

I can see out of the corner of my eye that she's standing next to my easel again. Some of the photos she took the other day are in her outstretched hand; I spot one of Zach laughing into the camera, holding the pan too high above the rusted stove. I don't look at Natalie's face, but she sounds uncertain, not quite sure what to say to me after I ran out of the pharmacy the other day.

I consider saying nothing, just acting like I didn't hear

her. She'll eventually have to give up and turn back to her work.

But after a pause that's a little too long, I decide to say hey back. My voice is dull. I don't look up.

"Was everything okay the other day?" Natalie asks. "You ran out and then you weren't at the car by the time I got there and your stuff was gone."

I could come up with something to tell her. I didn't feel well or I suddenly remembered that I had to be somewhere.

"Maybe we could do something tomorrow," Natalie says. We could.

But no, I decide. It would be better—easier—not to have plans with Natalie ever again. Otherwise it will only be harder to get back to my old routine, my normal life, when my mother comes home.

As I try to figure out what to tell Natalie, I think of Kelly in the sixth grade cafeteria again, making that gesture to her friend while I stood right behind them, seeing everything.

Somewhere inside me, I must have some of the same meanness that made Kelly able to look at me and do that. Right?

"I can't," I tell Natalie, trying to make my voice flat, not apologetic at all. "Sorry."

I can tell Natalie hears my tone. I look up and see her

turn away from me. Her cheeks go red. She stares down at her photos so intently I'm pretty sure she's not seeing them at all. I know that trick.

I'm sorry, I think at her. *I can't be the person you think I am.* But of course she can't read my mind.

If she could, she never would have wanted to be my friend in the first place.

———

I spend the rest of art dabbing my brush against the paper, creating shapeless watery blobs that look the way I feel, wishing it were any day but Thursday. Natalie and I are both supposed to work at Uncle John's office this afternoon.

When the bell rings, I clean up faster than I ever have before and rush through the halls to my locker. I don't need to pick up any books, but I stand there, locker door open, for at least five minutes. I drum my fingers against the metal and watch my neighbors grab their jackets and check their hair. I want to give Natalie a head start. I can walk to Uncle John's office from here.

I'm walking away from the school when Natalie drives past me. I see her cell phone next to her ear and wonder whether she's telling Zach what I said. I hope she isn't. Then I remind myself it doesn't matter. My brain cycles back and forth between those two thoughts—that I don't want Natalie and Zach to hate me; that I don't need to care what they think—for the entire walk to Uncle John's office.

When I get there, I see Natalie stationed at a computer on the other side of the room. I don't stop to see whether Claire wants me to help her.

I just cross straight to Uncle John's office, half-nodding at the few people who greet me. Uncle John isn't meeting with any clients, and I'm glad. I don't know where I would have gone if there had been people in his office.

Without thinking too much about what I'm doing, I drop into a seat at Uncle John's wooden table and dump my bag on the floor.

He looks up at the noise. "Hello, Sophie," he says. "How was your day?"

Exactly what I wanted my mother to ask me yesterday.

Uncle John smiles, the same open smile from last time, when I thought he was only being friendly because the Carter family was here.

That smile is all it takes to make me feel like a terrible person.

A terrible person who reaches deep down for the meanest things she can think of to tell someone else—her mother, her cousin, her new friend—and then says those things to that person's face.

A terrible person who wants her mother to stay in the

hospital just so her life can be a little more like everyone else's.

A terrible person who has felt relieved that, because her mother is in the hospital, she doesn't have to spend so much time worrying about her every day. Even though her mother is in the hospital because she tried to kill herself.

"Why are you being so nice to me?" is what comes out of my mouth.

Uncle John blinks. He shifts in his chair, looking uncomfortable and confused. I drop my head and stare down at the table, feeling tears gathering at the corners of my eyes again. What is wrong with me? I'm not a person who cries.

"Sophie? Are you all right?"

Still staring at the table, I shake my head. Then shrug. Then nod. Then I shrug again.

"So that would be a no," Uncle John says, and I let out a single dry, involuntary laugh. His hand waves a tissue under my nose, and I take it and dab at the corners of my eyes while trying to move as little as possible.

Then I give up and blow my nose loudly. It's not like Uncle John doesn't already know I'm upset.

"I don't expect you to tell me what's bothering you," he says. I stare at the table some more.

"You're just like your aunt that way," he adds, and I'm so surprised, I finally look up. "Both of you are convinced no one else really wants to know what's wrong and that you would be burdening them by telling, even when they ask you. Neither of you ever wants to clue other people in to what's going on in your head."

Me, just like Aunt Cynthia?

Uncle John stands up. "I mean that," he says. "People wouldn't ask if they didn't really want to know."

He walks over to the bookshelf and pulls a rolled up, rubber band–tied white bundle from the cluster against the shelves. When he comes back to the table, he smiles at me, more gently than before, almost as if he's asking whether the smile is okay with me.

"But I know not to hold my breath for a confession," he says. He shakes his head slightly, as if we mystify him, Aunt Cynthia and I.

He unrolls the sheets—not floor plans this time, but what looks like a diagram showing the elevations on one plot of land—and passes me books to weigh down the paper on my side of the table.

"Feel like doing some work?" he asks. I nod.

He hands me a notepad and pencil and explains what I'm looking at and what he needs me to do with it. I take careful notes, because I know I'm not focused enough to catch everything he's saying.

For the rest of the afternoon, the two of us work in silence, sketching on opposite sides of the table. I try not to think about Natalie, who is probably sitting outside fuming at me as she edits her photos on the computer. Uncle John pretends not to notice all the times I reach over for the box of tissues.

EIGHTEEN

BY THE TIME SCHOOL ENDS ON FRIDAY, I'M EXHAUSTED.

I'm tired of ignoring Natalie—not that she's tried to get my attention since yesterday. She spent art with her back to my easel, and she seemed to do a much better job of concentrating on her photos than I did on my painting.

I'm fed up with trying to avoid Leila and James, one of whom I seem to see in every hallway I walk through between classes. I'm tired of the horrible things I keep saying every time I open my mouth.

If I climbed into bed right now, I decide, I could sleep for a century. Or possibly longer. I could sleep the way my mother does in her hospital bed, with no awareness of the world around her.

But when I leave school, my feet don't take me toward Aunt Cynthia's, where I could nap all afternoon and no one would notice. They stride toward the hospital, and when my brain catches up, I realize I do want to see my mother. Not the mother I wished for a few days ago, the one who would sit me down with a snack after school and ask questions about my day, but my mother the way she actually is. The way she usually is in the afternoons, when I show up in her studio and she pulls me over to her easel to ask my opinion on her painting, or when she surprises me with a ride home from school.

The person she is completely apart from the moods that sometimes take over her life; the woman who can be so happy and in love with the world she makes it impossible not to be cheerful. The woman who always has time to explain an art technique I don't know and can come up with a creative project that will take my mind off of anything I don't want to think about.

As I walk, I remember the afternoon I came home from school and hurried down to my mother's studio, upset because Leila hadn't spoken to me in three or four days, since the beginning of sixth grade. It was longer than we'd gone without speaking since we were old enough to talk.

My mother put her paintbrush down and turned off her radio, not seeming to mind that I was interrupting her work.

"I'm sure Leila's just trying to figure out middle school, sweetie," she said when I told her what was going on. "It's confusing, with so many new classes and new people, and you know it's important to Leila to make a lot of friends."

I nodded. That had always been more important to Leila than to me.

"I'm sure she'll be herself again in a few days," my mother said. She made it sound so reasonable it was impossible not to believe her.

My mother never liked to stop painting when she was on fire with a project, but that day, she set her brush down and turned off the studio lamps, locked the door behind us, and pulled me upstairs and out to the car. We drove for two hours to get to the beach, where we waded straight into the water, still in our clothes, and had a splash war until I wasn't thinking about school or how weird Leila was being. I was just running and shrieking at the cold fall water and the way long strings of seaweed kept getting stuck between my toes, then trailing through the ocean behind me, like a dress with a wavy dark green train.

———

"I'm sorry."

This time I actually say it, instead of just thinking it the way I did to Natalie. I announce my apology as I walk into my mother's room, before I've even checked to see whether she's awake and listening.

"Sophie?" My mother is awake, and today she really does

169

sound more alert than she did before, with more inflection to her voice. But she also sounds puzzled, and I know, with the medications she's been on, that she doesn't remember much of our earlier conversation at all. Sometimes the combination of pills she has to take can leave her pretty out of it.

I'm not sure whether I want her to remember or not.

"I'm sorry about all the things I said the other day, Mom," I say again. "About you not caring how I am. I didn't mean—"

I'm about to say *I didn't mean it*. But that's not true. I meant all of it.

What I actually want to say is *I know it's not your fault that this is the way you are*. I know my mother can't do much about the way her genes tell her brain to work.

Sometimes I just wish her brain worked differently.

"It's okay," my mother says.

I still have no idea whether she remembers the things I said to her. Maybe she's accepting the apology just because I made it and she can see I mean it, whatever it's for. She sometimes does that when we argue, just lets me off the hook because she can tell how sorry I am.

I walk around to her other side, where the plastic hospital railing on her bed is already lowered. She pats the blanket next to her as if she's been saving me the spot.

I kick off my shoes and climb up, trying not to remember the last time I scrambled onto her bed, how absolutely still she was and the way I held her hand while we waited for the ambulance. I gripped her fingers so hard it would have hurt her if she'd been awake to feel it. But I don't think she even knew I was there.

As I sit, stretching my legs out parallel to hers, I realize I'm not done being angry. I haven't asked her how she's feeling today, and I don't particularly want to.

"Do you want to play a game?" I ask her instead. I'm still looking for a distraction. "I have that deck of cards."

"Maybe in a little while," she says.

Then she surprises me by reaching over and grabbing my hand. We sit in silence together for a minute, then two. It doesn't feel comfortable. It feels like my mother wants to say something but can't figure out how to start.

"I don't like being like this," she finally says.

Her voice is so quiet. I'm right next to her, and I still have to lean down to hear her better.

"I know, Mom," I start to say. But she squeezes my fingers and shakes her head to tell me she isn't finished yet. I'm surprised by how clear-headed and forceful she seems all of a sudden; how quickly the medication and therapy can work when the doctors are monitoring exactly what she's doing.

Again I feel that pang of guilt for not watching what she does that carefully.

For enjoying the past few days I've spent not watching her that carefully.

"I don't like being like this," she says again. "Except that, Sophie—sometimes I do like it. I like feeling as if I can do absolutely anything. And I know my work is better when I'm not on all these pills."

"But, Mom—" I start to interrupt. She squeezes my fingers a second time, murmurs *shh*. I wonder why she's chosen this moment to act like my parent again, holding my hand and making soft calming sounds. I tell myself I won't let any of it work on me the way she wants it to.

"But I know it's not better for you. So I just wanted to say that I'm going to try," she says. "To keep up with the pills and therapy and everything, and I know the doctor had some good suggestions about places that would be better with our insurance."

"He did," I manage. "He wrote it all down for me."

The piece of paper, with the name and address and phone number I still haven't looked at, is in the pocket of my other pair of jeans, on the floor of the guest room.

I'm going to try. My mother's words echo through my head, bouncing and shifting, and suddenly they're all mixed up with words she's said before. *I'm going to take my pills,*

172

Sophie, but just in case I forget sometimes, I want you to remind me. You can do that, right?

I can do that, I told her when I was eleven. I took it seriously, the job of reminding her to take her medicine every morning before I left for school.

She took the pills nearly every day for five years.

And then, one week, she stopped.

Now, on the bed, I squeeze her hand back and look over at her. She's completely convinced that she'll remember the pills forever this time, that she'll force herself to take them every day, even if they make her hands shake too much for her to sketch or her head feel too fuzzy for her to paint. Even if she misses a few nights' sleep, suddenly feels happier and more capable than she can ever remember being before, and starts to wonder why she's taking pills if she's absolutely fine.

I don't believe her.

But I also know, looking at her, that she's certain she's telling the truth. And that version of my mother—not the impossible afternoon-snack-at-the-kitchen-table Mom but the trying-to-stay-on-solid-ground Mom, the Mom who drives me to the beach and runs with me through the waves—is the one I have to hope I get back.

Even if that means I have to give up some other things.

And for one moment, I'm sure I've made the right decision.

I need to go back to my old, Mom-centric life, the one where I go straight home after school every day, do my homework, make dinner, and spend my free time on the worn cushion in the corner of my mother's studio, keeping her company while she paints and pretends to have a secret life as an orchestra conductor.

While she takes medication, goes to therapy, and tries to keep her moods in check so that my life will be as stable as possible.

I lean toward my mother, move some hair away from her face, and kiss her cheek.

"I'll see you soon, Mom," I say. "I'll probably be back tomorrow. Want me to bring you anything?"

She shakes her head. I try to slide off the bed without messing up the blankets, and when my feet touch the ground, I let go of her hand.

"Bye, Sophie," she says. She blows a kiss, loud and exaggerated, into the air. I hold up my hand and catch it.

And I'm not even sure why, but as I tug the yellow curtain closed and leave her room, I actually feel a little bit better.

NINETEEN

SATURDAY MORNING AGAIN.

But this time, when the alarm *beep beep beeps* me awake even earlier than last week, I don't hit the snooze button. Instead, I climb out of bed, get dressed quickly, and open the guest room window to let in the breeze I can see brushing against the leaves outside. They're just beginning to change color.

I pull out the notes and half a sketch I made in Uncle John's office on Thursday, sit cross-legged behind the desk, and start to draw.

One of Uncle John's projects is a house for a family moving here from California. They bought a huge plot of land with a creek, he told me, and they want to build a house there from scratch. Something that will keep the cold out but let them see the sun, the way they could from their old house.

175

"See whether you can come up with anything," Uncle John told me, passing over a few architecture magazines full of glossy photos. "Maybe these will give you some ideas. Just sketch whatever you can think of. Don't worry about the format or anything, we're just looking for a starting point."

He was probably only trying to distract me and didn't really need the help, but as I drifted off to sleep last night, I couldn't stop thinking about the family and their sunlit house. Now, as I stare at the tree just outside the window, I remember my mother's favorite house too, the one with the wide windows and glass doors, standing out among all the nearby farms. I turn the pages of Uncle John's magazines, looking at all the houses with balconies and the ones that look out on lakes. Somehow, the photos calm me and clear my head.

By the time Uncle John knocks on the door to see if I'm ready to go to the office, I have a rough sketch finished. The design is modern and angular, like the shapes I draw when I'm doodling, but this time they mean something. I imagine the first floor's entire back wall made of glass and a wide balcony stretching around one of the corners of the second floor. Near the edge of the page I draw the creek, with a wooden bench facing the water.

When I close my eyes, I can see the California family

there, even though I have no idea what they look like. I see the kids throwing sticks into the creek and walking back and forth across the water, balancing on stones, while their parents sit on the deck with the newspapers, eating fruit out of a big yellow bowl.

The way I imagine them there isn't so different from the way my mother imagines us, moving into her favorite house and finding a way to make each room ours.

———

Even once Uncle John and I have gone over my sketch, combining it with his version and brainstorming more ideas, there are still a few hours of work left. And I know I won't be able to avoid Natalie all day.

I follow Uncle John over to the filing cabinets and table near Claire's desk, each of us carrying a heavy stack of papers. Natalie is working at a computer right next to us, but after I set my stack down, I turn back to Uncle John without looking at her.

"Are you all set with this stuff?" Uncle John asks me.

I nod. It's just collating and stapling.

He glances from me to Natalie and back again, and I wonder if he's noticed that we haven't said hello to each other this morning.

But now he just nods at both of us and turns away with a "Come find me if you need anything, either of you."

We work in a silence so deep that every time I staple something, I jump at the clacking sound. If Natalie were talking to me, she would probably mock me for it. But whenever I look over in quick glances that I try to make as unobvious as possible, she's listening to her music and seems totally focused on the screen in front of her.

I wonder if she's pretending or if she's already completely stopped caring that I'm here.

Just as I staple my next stack of papers, Natalie's computer dings, the sound of an instant message. After a few seconds, she lets out a soft huff of a laugh. Then I hear the keys clicking quickly, loudly, as she types something back. The rest of the room is silent.

I wonder if she's chatting with Zach, or if the person on the other end is one of her other friends from school. A real friend, one who actually got to the stage of friendship where she and Natalie traded phone numbers and called each other to hang out. Maybe she's already forgotten that the afternoon with James and me and Zach at the abandoned house even happened.

Natalie laughs again and types some more. We still haven't said a word to each other today.

I suddenly see myself from above, an aerial shot of the girl sitting alone in front of her locker, standing by herself at work. But instead of seeing her and thinking *productive* or *industrious*, I think *sad*.

Then I wonder if this is how my mother feels when her moods shift, *snap*, just like that?

Twenty-four hours ago, I was walking out of my mother's room feeling more upbeat than I had since the moment I found her lying motionless on her bed that day after school. I was certain yesterday that I was okay with what would happen to us next. My mother would come home, get treatment, take her pills day after day. I would be there, just like before, to nag her about it and keep her company. Our old, familiar trade.

But now—*snap*—as I stand by the filing cabinets, stapling furiously and listening to Natalie laugh at a joke I'm not in on, I feel as though my stomach is about to curl in on itself.

Suddenly, I'm just as sure that my plan of spending my days with my mother, climbing up and down from her studio to our small apartment with the cheerful orange kitchen, won't be enough at all.

———

The nurses at the hospital are starting to recognize me, and when I stop by the front desk on Saturday evening, I only get out the first syllable of my last name before one of them hands me a pass for the eighth floor.

"It's okay," she waves me on with a smile. "Go right up."

But when I get close to my mother's room upstairs, I stop. There are people talking inside.

Did my mother get a roommate in the last twenty-four hours? Or is there a doctor or a nurse with her?

But I know that's not it—both voices sound too familiar.

I stand just outside the door, tracing my finger over the letters on Tanya Wilson's plaque again, trying to hear the murmured conversation. One of the people speaking is definitely my mother. But the other one?

"I'm sorry I didn't explain it to her," the second voice says. It's lower than my mother's, but something about it, maybe the way the speaker emphasizes certain words, is similar. "None of what happened was her fault."

"Of course it wasn't," my mother answers. "It was my fault."

"No, Amy." The second voice again, and the way it says my mother's name with soft affection and sadness rings a bell in my head. *I know, Amy, I know.*

The second voice continues, and now it sounds shakier and thicker. I wonder if whoever is speaking has started crying.

"I don't blame you either," my mother's visitor says. "I was just so angry, not to mention scared for my daughter. I made a decision on my own because I didn't think talking about it with you would do any good."

My finger stops tracing the letters on the plaque in the middle of the *i*. My hand hovers there, frozen over the dot.

I know the second voice; it's Aunt Cynthia's.

I picture her sitting there by my mother's bed, looking neat in the lightweight yellow sweater and jeans she had on this morning, tiny colored glass earrings in her ears and her hair pinned back away from her face. Maybe she's holding my mother's hand, the way I did yesterday. Or maybe she's sitting farther away, twisting her rings around on her fingers, glancing at and then away from my mother as they talk.

Has she been coming here all this time, and we've just missed each other? Or is this her first visit? If it is, why is she here now?

More questions pile on top of one another in my head. What are she and my mother talking about? What did Aunt Cynthia need to explain, and who did she not explain it to? What decision did she make without consulting my mother?

I try to lean closer without making it possible for them to see me.

After a moment, my mother says, "Of course you wouldn't think talking about it would do any good, Cynthia."

She sounds knowing, warm, and exasperated all at the same time as she adds, "You never want to talk about anything you're thinking or feeling."

Uncle John's words pop into my head. *You're just like your aunt that way.*

My mother is still talking, and her voice now is softer and more strained, as if she's pulling each word out of herself letter by letter.

"But it doesn't feel right that you don't talk to me about my own...situation," my mother says, hesitating over the last word. "It makes me feel like you're making all the decisions for me. Like I'm just an illness and not a person."

Like I'm just an illness and not a person.

I stand there in the hallway, stunned at the words, and I imagine Aunt Cynthia must be too, because it feels like several minutes before she responds, and she sounds surprised.

"I'm sorry," she says again. "I didn't even..." she trails off. I picture her shaking her head, the way she does sometimes when she's thinking. "I never thought about that, but you're right."

"Of course I'm right," my mother says. Her voice sounds clear now.

Then, suddenly, my mother and Aunt Cynthia are laughing. I stand in the hallway with my ear practically flattened against the wall of the room, listening as their soft giggles become loud, full laughs.

In a flash, I see them again the way Uncle John described them to me: best friends sharing their first apartment in the city, throwing parties and trading clothes and cooking dinner together. They giggle as they toss all the spices in their cabinets into the pots simmering on their stove, twirling each other around the kitchen. When they argue, stomping off into their own rooms, they come out quickly to forgive each other.

Without stepping into my mother's room, I turn around and hurry down the hall, more confused than before. My mother thinks Aunt Cynthia treats her more as an illness than a person. Do I do the same thing?

I get off the elevator on the second floor and make a right into the cafeteria. It's not that I want to eat hospital food; the cookies and wilted salads here don't look much better than the wriggly desserts and mystery meat my mother gets upstairs.

But I'm definitely not ready to go back to Aunt Cynthia's house.

I buy a cup of tea and find a table in the back corner, where I open my sketchbook and stare at it without taking out a pencil. I flip through the pages slowly, the story of my last week—the Carters' land and house, the drawing of my feet by my mother's bed—until I land on a blank sheet. Then I have nothing to focus on but the thoughts in my head.

Why was Aunt Cynthia here? What did she mean when

she said she made a decision because she was scared for her daughter—for Leila? Why does she seem to regret that decision all of a sudden?

The same questions I had upstairs, ceaselessly circling in my head.

I think of the last time my mother, Leila, and I were together, that day in August right before Leila and I started middle school, when we went out driving with my mother. The afternoon we spent playing with our dolls in the backseat while my mother sang along to the country radio station, strands of her hair moving in the breeze from the window.

My mother turned around in the front seat with a game for us, a challenge issued in her high-speed secret code voice. *How fast?*

It was just like any other game we played. So why did everything change?

———

"It's Sophie, right?"

I jump, sloshing my tea. I'm certain Aunt Cynthia has somehow found me here in this empty corner of the cafeteria. I don't know what to say to her about what I overheard.

But when I look up, it isn't Aunt Cynthia—it's Uncle John's client, Trudy Carter. The one whose mother has been in and out of the hospital.

"Hi, Sophie? I'm not sure if you remember me—your uncle is designing my family's new house. We met last time we saw him to discuss the plans," Trudy says, her voice rising at the end like it's a question. "You took notes for us?"

"Of course," I say.

She's right next to my table, so I stand up quickly and shake her hand. Then I wave at the empty chair across from me, even though I don't really want Trudy to take it. She sits down, setting a plastic-wrapped chocolate chip cookie and a cup of coffee in front of her.

I watch as she pulls the coffee close and drinks, practically planting her face in the cup.

"Sorry," she says after a long sip. She sighs. "It's been that kind of day."

I nod, thinking of how impossibly tired I've felt since yesterday. Since my mother got here, actually. The tea isn't helping.

I don't really know what to say to Trudy, so I just wait for her to keep talking, my arms resting on the table, crossed over the blank open pages of my sketchbook.

"Last time your uncle called us about the house, he said you were the one who came up with most of the ideas for my mother's suite," Trudy says after a few more sips of coffee. She unwraps her cookie, takes a bite, makes a face.

I shrug. "My uncle asked me to help him brainstorm."

"Well, we all really liked what you came up with," she says. "I even brought the plans upstairs to show my mother just now. She was nervous about leaving her own place, and I think your plans made her feel better about it."

"Really?" I ask.

My voice comes out eager and surprised, and I feel a strange warmth in my chest at the idea that the plans I thought up with Uncle John helped Trudy and her mother. Fixed something for them. For a moment I forget all about my mother and Aunt Cynthia and my confusion.

"Really," Trudy says. She smiles at me.

I think about telling her that my mother is here too, upstairs on the eighth floor. That I know exactly how tired she feels. But what could Trudy, a stranger, tell me that I don't already know?

So I sit there quietly while Trudy sips her coffee and wraps up the rest of her cookie. I can tell that her attention has drifted away, so I pull a pencil from my bag and start filling the blank page in front of me. I look up only when Trudy's chair scrapes back from the table. I didn't want her to join me, but I'm actually glad she did.

"I'm sure I'll see you again," Trudy says, and I nod.

"Next month," I say, wondering if I could get Natalie in trouble for this. "My friend took some photos of your house, and they'll be in a show at the arts center. In case you want to come see it."

I'm not sure why I choose this moment, now that I'm not talking to her, to call Natalie my friend. And I'm not sure how I know that Trudy would like the photos and wouldn't mind that we sneaked into the house to take them. But Trudy smiles and thanks me, and I hope she really does come, so she can see someone else's idea of what her house could be.

———

Trudy isn't the right person to talk to about my mother, but as I leave the hospital and start back toward Aunt Cynthia's, I realize there is someone else who might be. I change direction, toward the four streets of stores and restaurants that make up our suburban downtown. The whole way, I keep my fingers crossed that the person I'm looking for will be there at 6:30 on a Saturday evening.

He is.

When I step into the pizza parlor, where booths with blue plastic benches line both walls and there's a line five people deep in front of the counter, James is behind the register taking people's orders and collecting money. Even with his paper pizza parlor hat on, I realize it's silly for me to pretend I don't think he's cute, because I do. I actually even like the hat.

I don't want pizza, but I wait anyway, behind two parents holding their toddler's hands between them. As the parents talk to each other over his head, the kid rests his weight on their arms and takes tiny jumps off the floor. One, two, three—jump. One, two, three—jump.

As the line creeps forward, I watch the families and groups of friends who fill the booths. I think of James finding me in the hallway last week and waiting for me to start talking instead of going in for band. Following me from English to art to ask if I was okay. I remember the question I wouldn't let him finish asking me the other day in Leila's room. And I repeat to myself what Uncle John told me the other day in his office.

You're convinced no one else really wants to know what's wrong, even when they ask you. But they really do.

Maybe they really do, I tell myself. *They really do.* I'm practically whispering it out loud as the toddler in front of me swings from his parents' hands, back and forth, back and forth. *I guess I'll find out.*

The parents grab their pizza and find a table, the dad giving the little boy a boost into his seat. And now I'm at the front of the line.

"Sophie." James sounds surprised to see me. He clears his throat. "Hi."

The last time I saw him, James had just watched me yell

at Leila and fling a grease-drenched paper plate across her room.

"Hi," I answer. I stare down at the counter.

I've just realized I have no idea what to say next. I was so busy reminding myself of Uncle John's words that I forgot to come up with some for myself. Now I'm jittery and nervous. What am I doing here?

I consider pretending I'm only here to buy a slice. That way I can order it and leave, shove the door open and walk away as fast as possible.

Instead I force myself to say, "I know you're working, but do you have a few minutes?" I gesture toward one of the few empty tables. "I can wait if now's not a good time."

James checks behind me—there's no one else in line—and then over at the clock.

"I can probably take my break now," he says. He doesn't comment on how weird it is for me to show up like this, and I appreciate it. "Let me just make sure."

He disappears into the back for what feels like fifteen minutes but is really only three or four. When he comes back, his paper pizza parlor hat is off and he's carrying a plate with two slices on it. One pepperoni, one veggie.

He steps through the door at the side of the counter and offers me the plate.

"Want one? I know how much you like veggie pizza."

James grins at me, and in spite of myself, I have to smile at what I know he's remembering: Leila's and my sixth birthday party. Just as I'm thinking about it, James starts telling me the story. It's the kind of story families tell—the kind of story the parents in front of me in line would probably tell everyone they knew if their little boy were the one in it—but I haven't heard anyone in my family tell it in a long time.

"We were all sitting at that table your uncle had set up in the backyard, remember?" James asks. "My parents came with me too, and some of the other kids from our class and their parents. And you and Leila were sitting there with your birthday hats, trying not to look too impatient for the cake and presents."

I remember just how impatient we were, me sitting there holding my fork upright; Leila looking over at the pile of presents every couple of minutes and then trying to pretend she was looking at something else. Every time my mother caught Leila looking, she would tease her about adding another minute onto the time before we could start opening the boxes.

"Your aunt gave you a slice of veggie pizza and you decided you didn't like it, but instead of saying anything, you just picked all the veggies off the plate, got up, and buried them in your aunt's garden. You dug a little hole and dumped them in."

"So they would decompose," I say like that should be obvious.

James laughs. "You were always into science and stuff," he agrees. This is why I'm here, because the way James knows me has nothing to do with my mother. He just knows me: that I've always liked science. That I'm still an artist. That sometimes I choose to bury my vegetables.

He holds the plate toward me again to make sure I still don't want any.

"No thanks," I tell him, holding my hands in front of me to ward away the vegetables. I'm surprised how easily the retort comes, like it hasn't been years since we've had this kind of conversation. "There's nowhere to put those veggies around here. Too much concrete."

He laughs again, and for some reason I blush. *What am I doing?* James follows me outside, eating as we go. The bells on the small strip hanging from the door jingle behind us as we leave.

We walk without speaking for a block, and it's like the memory we were sharing gradually fades away and the tension from the last few times we've seen each other rushes back in its place. At the corner, we both turn, toward the train station and the diner on the next corner, and keep going, our steps nearly synchronized. I'm thinking about the story James just told me. I'd almost forgotten that day, the way we all sat there, laughing and eating off of pink and purple plates and opening presents and taking pictures. It was just...a normal day. Just like the day we spent with Natalie and Zach. Suddenly, I can remember a dozen others we had, with James and without him.

Finally, in front of the town green, I stop walking. There are benches and a rotating series of statues here, the current one a brightly colored twist of metal that looks, when I tilt my head a certain way, like a woman dancing, balanced on her toes. Ms. Triste brought the sculptor into class, so when I look at the statue, I see her, an older woman with a long gray braid down her back.

I don't sit down, and I don't turn to face James. All I can manage is to stare at the ground and talk.

"My mother's in the hospital," I say. "She has been since the fourth day of school. She tried to kill herself by OD'ing on pills."

I hear myself, abrupt and matter-of-fact, like I'm just opening my mouth and letting the words drop heavily to the ground. I'm not trying to sound like that, but it's the only way I know to get the sentences out. Just let them fall.

"You were wondering why I'm staying at Leila's house now." I hardly ever say my cousin's name out loud, and it feels strange coming out of my mouth. "That's why. And why I seemed kind of out of it." Because that's exactly how I've been feeling.

James says nothing for a long moment.

Finally, twisting my empty hands together in front of me, I look up at him.

He's staring at me, the plate held forgotten at an angle in his hand. Then he says, "Holy shit, Soph."

And I know in a rush; Uncle John was right.

"Yeah, exactly," I agree, pushing down an odd impulse to laugh. Instead I nod toward the pizza that's starting to slide off James's plate. Then I reach over and straighten it, my hand brushing against his arm. My face reddens.

I turn and start to walk, and James's steps keep up. We're making a square around town, back toward the pizza parlor.

I don't say anything else, waiting for James to follow up, to ask me whatever he wants to know. But the only sounds are our sneakers scraping the sidewalk in a rhythm much steadier than I feel.

Then I get it. James has already asked me questions, those times in the hallway and this week when he came over to work on the project and saw me sitting on Leila's floor with messy hair and red eyes. Now it's my turn to decide whether and how I want to answer him. Whether I want to let him into what's going on in my head.

So I take a deep breath and begin.

"My mother has bipolar disorder," I tell him. The words still come out steady and clinical even though the trampoline jumpers are back to their routine in my stomach, bouncing to a rhythm of *what will he think, what will he think*. "That means she can have pretty serious mood swings, and a lot of times bipolar people attempt suicide when they're manic or in a mixed state, because that's when they have the energy to act on suicidal thoughts. That's why she overdosed."

"I had no idea," James says, and when I glance over, he's shaking his head slowly back and forth, looking stunned. I believe him.

But that means everything I thought about why he and Leila stopped speaking to me no longer makes sense.

"I thought you knew," I say.

"No," James says again. "What made you think that?" He turns and starts to walk backward, facing me. And he really does look like he wants to know. His whole body is loose and open, here, waiting.

I look down and slow my pace, shuffling my feet. My stomach turns over. I wish I could melt into the sidewalk and become one of those little bumps in the concrete. That would be easier than talking about this.

"When we stopped hanging out in middle school," I

194

mumble. "I figured it was because you guys thought my mother was crazy."

"Wait, what?" James stops abruptly and sticks his arm out to the side, as if to keep me from trying to make a break for it. He doesn't need to stop me. I'm already standing completely still.

"I never thought that," James says. "I thought you didn't want to hang out with us."

"But you didn't—" I start. Then stop. "Leila was the one who—"

I glance at James again. He looks confused. I feel confused, and all I can do is shake my head the way he did a moment ago. I don't understand. Didn't he see Kelly making fun of me and just sit there not doing anything about it because he thought Kelly was right? Didn't he choose not to call me back?

We both start walking again then, as if we've agreed standing there isn't helping. When we get back to the pizza parlor, James continues right past the door, even though I'm sure his break must be almost over.

"Then why did we stop hanging out?" I ask. As much as I don't want to talk about it, it also feels important that I know the answer.

"I guess I don't know," James says, his voice low. "You never came and sat with us at lunch after sixth grade started, and I didn't really go over to Leila's house after school anymore, and I just thought..." He trails off. "I don't know what I thought. I just assumed you'd decided you wanted to find some new friends. Lots of people in middle school did."

He doesn't sound bothered by it now, but I suddenly picture his smaller self, skinny and floppy-haired, wondering what I was doing. *Were you upset?* I almost want to ask. I want to know what was going through his head, and suddenly I have an idea how he might have felt the past few days, asking me questions I refused to answer.

We turn the corner again toward the station and the green.

"Did something happen?" James asks. "Back then, I mean, with Leila? To make you guys stop hanging out."

"I don't know," I say, but it's so soft I'm not sure James even hears me. I think of that last summer, before sixth grade, playing with Leila and my mother every day. What am I missing?

"Maybe you should talk to her," James offers, as if he's answering my mental question. "She seemed pretty upset after the other day. Even though you guys don't hang out anymore, you're still kind of on the same wavelength most of the time."

"Maybe," I say. James has spent hardly any time with both of us together in the last five years, but somehow he's right.

Leila and I usually are on the same wavelength in a way. We're like two trains taking the same route on tracks that never touch, that stretch parallel to each other all the way until the last stop.

But then I think about the way I yelled at Leila the other day and raged out of her room. I don't feel ready to talk to her yet. I'm not sure when I will be.

Instead of completing the square again, I turn around, and James follows me back to the pizza place. He pulls the door open, the bells jangling again, and I start to walk away.

"Hey, Soph?" James calls from behind me. I turn back. "That really sucks about your mom. I'm sorry. I know there probably isn't much, but let me know if there's anything I can do."

He pauses for a minute. "Your mom was always pretty cool, you know. I mean, my stick figures would all still have *really* long torsos if she hadn't taught me about proportions."

Despite everything, then, I laugh. James looks absurdly pleased, like that was the effect he was going for. He stands there, one hand on the door of the pizza place, watching as I turn around to leave.

And I start to think that it's not just Uncle John who was right; maybe Natalie was too.

TWENTY

WHEN I WAKE UP ON SUNDAY, THE HOUSE IS UNUSUALLY still, the kind of quiet so noticeable it feels even louder than sound. Where is everyone?

Without changing out of my pajamas, I pad downstairs toward the kitchen to hunt for a bagel. My stomach is rumbling. I never ate dinner after I left James at the pizza parlor last night. By the time my brain stopped replaying his words—*let me know if there's anything I can do; your mom was always pretty cool, you know*—I wasn't hungry.

Now, just outside the kitchen doorway, I stop. Aunt Cynthia is there at the counter, chopping something on a cutting board and humming so softly I couldn't hear it from the hall. For a moment she looks like my mother, lost in her own world, chopping and swaying to whatever song she's half humming aloud, half hearing in her head.

The weirdness of it—the ways Aunt Cynthia is like my mother, the ways my mother can never be like her—hits me and I take a sharp breath. Aunt Cynthia must hear it, because the chopping stops abruptly.

"Sophie?" she calls. "That you?"

I step into the kitchen. "I'm sorry, I just came down to get a bagel. I didn't mean to interrupt."

"Of course you're not interrupting," Aunt Cynthia says. But she doesn't seem surprised that I would think so. She sounds almost sad, like she's sorry for making me feel like I was interrupting. She turns and points her chopping knife at the bread drawer where the bagels are.

"Leila and your uncle are out," she adds. That explains why it's so quiet.

I take a bagel and butter it, and then, because Aunt Cynthia's still watching me, her knife poised over her cutting board but not actually chopping, I pour a glass of juice and sit down at the table instead of going back upstairs. I hear Aunt Cynthia's knife start up again. I eat quickly. Chew, swallow, sip.

At least a full minute later, Aunt Cynthia says, "I saw your mother yesterday."

"I know," I say, before I realize I'll have to explain myself.

"I was on my way to visit her when I heard the two of you talking," I add. "I didn't want to barge in on your visit, so I left without going in." I don't tell her how long I stood outside the room, eavesdropping, before I left.

Aunt Cynthia scrapes whatever she's been chopping into a bowl, then rinses the cutting board and knife and thuds them into the sink. I get the feeling she's stretching out the task as long as she can. Maybe she's stalling while she tries to figure out what to say next.

At last she dries her hands, walks over to the table, and pulls out the chair across from me. She stares down at the tabletop, still silent, and I think again of what Uncle John said about the ways she and I are alike. Is that why it's easier for me to talk to Natalie and Zach and Trudy and Uncle John, why it used to be easier for me to talk to Leila and James, but I have so much trouble talking to Aunt Cynthia? Because, out of all of them, she's the most like me?

Even now, it feels like there's a wall across the middle of the table, a stone structure we can't see the top of and that neither of us knows how to climb over. A wall like the one in my head, blocking away all the phrases about my mother that I don't want to let out.

As we sit here in silence, staring down, I realize just how many questions I have. Questions James or Trudy or any of those other people wouldn't be able to answer. I want to ask Aunt Cynthia why she stopped coming over when I was in middle school. Why she started telling me her daughter couldn't come to the phone every time I called. Why they all left me alone with my mother for so many years. Whether my mother has always been the way she is now.

I think of the way Uncle John described the younger Aunt Cynthia to me, as the woman he met at my mother's party and didn't want to stop talking to. And then there's the way I've started to imagine her: sharing my mother's clothes, dancing with her in the kitchen the same way she and Leila and I used to do. I take that image of Aunt Cynthia and try to place it over the one I know now, like one of those books James used to have with pictures on clear plastic sheets so we could put the layers of a building together one by one.

I try to hold all of Aunt Cynthia's layers in my mind at once. Then I take a deep breath, look over that imaginary wall in the middle of the table, and take a running leap.

Even so, when I get to the other side, what I say surprises me.

"Were you ever scared it would happen to you?" I hear myself ask. "That you would go crazy too?"

I know *crazy* isn't the right term, isn't the word I would want anyone else to use when talking about my mother. Isn't the word I wanted Kelly to be thinking that day at the lunch table. But right now I don't want the clinical, politically correct terms, *bipolar* or *manic-depressive*. I want to know whether Aunt Cynthia has ever been scared that she would lose her mind.

Aunt Cynthia looks up and meets my eyes.

"Yes," she says, just like that. She drops the word onto the table the same way I explained my mother's situation to James yesterday. *Yes.*

I'm oddly relieved, as if Aunt Cynthia's answer is confirmation that I'm not crazy.

Then the next question, the flip side of that one, the thing I haven't dared to ask Dr. Choi or any of the nurses I've met by my mother's bed. "Do you think she'll ever get better? I mean, completely better, not just for a few months or years the way she usually does?"

Aunt Cynthia smiles a small, sad smile that I recognize. It's the same one I saw on Trudy's face yesterday, and the one I smiled back at her. Aunt Cynthia stretches out her hand as if she wants to pat mine, but the wall is still there—maybe an inch or two shorter, but there—and she doesn't reach all the way to my side of the table.

"I don't know," she says softly, and I nod.

I'm not disappointed; that's what I expected her to say. I finish chewing and lean forward in my chair, about to push it back and get up.

"But I don't think we should hold our breath for that to happen," Aunt Cynthia says. Her voice is softer, and she's looking back down at the table; I'm not sure she's really talking to me at all.

I lean back again.

"I'm not holding my breath," I tell her. "I know there isn't any kind of cure right now." *I've talked to the doctors more recently than you have* is what I mean but don't say. How can she think she needs to be telling me this?

"That's not what I'm talking about," Aunt Cynthia says. She shakes her head, frustrated she can't find the right words. Even when she isn't in court or writing a legal brief, she always chooses her words carefully. It's something my mother used to tease her about, how long it would sometimes take her to get one of her thoughts out. "I mean we shouldn't put everything on hold until some far-off day when she might get better. And we shouldn't make all our decisions based on the fact that she might not either. It's not our job to do that."

Aunt Cynthia pushes her chair back and stands up, her palms planted on the table. I want to ask her if that's what she was doing five years ago, when she first left my mother and me alone—choosing to stop putting what she wanted on hold. I want to ask what was so important she had to cut us off like that.

But before I can ask those questions, she's at the counter again, back to business, mixing some kind of sauce for her vegetables. Conversation over. I get up too.

As I walk back upstairs, my feet slapping against the wood floors, I wonder whether that's what I was doing when I told Natalie I didn't want to hang out. Whether that's what my mother and I have been doing all this time, reining our real selves in; my mother taking her medication to stay normal for me, me sketching on her studio floor and keeping her company when I could have been out with my own friends. Whether we've been putting ourselves on hold for each other.

———

I spend the rest of Sunday losing myself in math. I read the week's textbook chapter and, one by one, finish all of the problems from class that I was too exhausted to do last week. Then I pull out a fresh sheet of graph paper and start the weekend's problem set. I draw each graph carefully, as if I'm doing them in pen instead of with a pencil I can erase.

When I finish the last problem, something about the final graph, a sine function, looks familiar. I trace my fingers over the curves that curl across the page like waves, and I realize I could bring a copy to Dr. Choi for my mother's medical file, because the graph looks like her life. She travels back and forth between 1 and -1, up and down and up. And I'm the axis, steady at zero.

I open my sketchbook, flipping the pages with my thumb until I get to the drawing I started last week of my mother lying asleep in her hospital bed, my falling-apart sneakers just poking into the corner of the picture. In small but blocky letters I start writing trigonometric equations along her blanket, parallel to her body, the way Mr. Borakov writes problems on the chalkboard in math class. I line them up, one after the other, until it's impossible to see where each one ends.

When I get to the bottom of the blanket, I lean back in my chair and look over what I've done. The rows of numbers, letters, symbols, and equals signs don't look much like math problems anymore. Even I can't separate them all, and when they run together they're more like a caption. They explain everything that's going on in the picture, but only to those who know what values to plug in.

TWENTY-ONE

IN ENGLISH CLASS ON MONDAY, MR. JACKSON HAS dragged an empty table to the front of the room, between his desk and ours. The group presentations start today.

I glance across the room at James and Leila. We still have a week to come up with our project, but we haven't spoken about it since the night I stormed out of Leila's room.

James looks back at me and grins. I selfishly hope the first group's project isn't good enough to make ours—whatever it ends up being—seem too terrible in comparison.

The group, three boys and a girl, sets up at the front of the room, the boys lifting a large cardboard box onto the table while the girl reviews the presentation notes she's made on index cards. The boys take something out of the box and set it down.

A few of my classmates give each other puzzled looks as

they figure out what the object on the table is: an old white microwave. There's something typed on the front—it looks like a poem printed on clear plastic labels and stuck to the door. Whoever put the labels on did it unevenly, slapping each verse down slightly askew below the previous one.

The girl at the front of the room clears her throat.

"We decided to do our project on Sylvia Plath," she says. "Plath was a poet, obviously, since this is the poetry unit, but she was also the author of a novel, *The Bell Jar*, which was first published in 1963. Plath was born in 1932, and…"

My mind wanders as the girl recites a few more dates from Plath's life, then passes the stack of note cards to another group member, who reads one of Plath's poems to the class. I tune back in when there's a hollow thudding sound. The last group member has slapped his hand against the top of the microwave.

"And now for the *creative* part of the project," the boy says.

Mr. Jackson chuckles from the back of the classroom, where he's been watching with his arms crossed, leaning against another table.

"Aside from her poems and novels themselves, one of the things Sylvia Plath is most known for is the fact that after several battles with depression in her twenties, she committed suicide at age thirty…" the boy pauses to press a button on the front of the microwave, and the door opens with a pop. A few people around me laugh.

"...By sticking her head in the gas oven in her own kitchen."

Oh God.

The boy at the front of the room is saying something about the Sylvia Plath effect and studies showing that poets are more prone to mental illness than other people, but I'm not really processing any of it. My brain is buzzing too loudly.

Taped to the back of the microwave above a layer of crusty food stains is a photo of what must be Sylvia Plath's face.

She has dark eyes and dark hair just past her shoulders, and from the part of her outfit that's visible, she's wearing some kind of shirt or cardigan with extra-large buttons. She looks young, except for the expression on her face. She's staring straight into the camera that took the photo—straight out at us—and she isn't smiling.

I think it takes me several minutes to wrench my eyes away from hers. Once I do, I stare down at my desk, but I can't stop seeing Sylvia Plath's face there. I blink and it turns into my mother's face, looking up at me with that same bold gaze. With almost the same dark eyes and hair. The two switch back and forth; Plath, my mother, Plath gazing out from the back of a grungy white microwave. I can't think.

I wonder hazily whether I'm going to throw up right now in class, in front of everyone.

It's definitely possible.

From somewhere in the room I hear a scraping noise, like several people are dragging their chairs out and standing up. Then I hear Leila's voice, which sounds, oddly, like it's coming closer to my side of the classroom. I look up and watch as she walks toward Mr. Jackson, carrying her books.

"Mr. Jackson, I'm so sorry," she's saying, "but I just realized James and Sophie and I promised to meet with the band director this period about a concert we're doing this weekend at the nursing home. It's crunch time for rehearsals, so he wanted to pull us out of the period before band today for a little extra practice." She waves a yellow slip of paper in Mr. Jackson's direction. It's the same rough size as a hall pass.

"None of us have study halls we can use for practice time," she adds, almost managing to sound sorry.

I'm not in band, and I'm pretty sure Leila and James aren't doing a concert at a nursing home any time soon. But I don't think Mr. Jackson knows that.

Without checking the paper, Mr. Jackson waves one hand in Leila's direction, telling her to go. I get up, grab my bag, and follow her, not taking my eyes off the floor again until I'm out in the hallway. Somehow, I stumble and fall against the nearest wall of lockers.

Leila and James each grab one of my arms and start to steer me down the hall.

"We're not really going to the band room, are we?" I ask. My voice sounds like it's coming from somewhere else, far away from my body. *I don't play an instrument* I almost add, but another part of my brain reminds me that they know that.

"Of course we're not," Leila says, but she doesn't sound exasperated or annoyed the way I expect. "We're going straight home."

Home. I know she means Aunt Cynthia's house, and I think of its large kitchen with the spotless stainless steel oven. I can't turn my brain off, can't keep myself from imagining what it would be like to walk into the kitchen and see Sylvia Plath in front of the oven, door open, head inside. Her chin would rest on the bottom metal rack, which Leila left in the perfect position for baking cookies.

"It'll be okay," James murmurs next to me. Leila mutters something that sounds like, "Fuck those guys." On my other side, she's shaking with fury.

James and Leila guide me down the steps, along the science hall, and out a side door, which locks behind us. We walk slowly across the lot to Leila's car, and I feel a flash of relief that she always parks in the back lot, where no one from the main office could possibly see us, even if they looked out the window at exactly this moment.

James opens the passenger door, his hand gently guiding me as I climb in, and he and Leila both stand there until I've buckled my seat belt. I don't have the energy to tell them not to hover.

James gets into the backseat and Leila starts the car, and for once she turns the radio down as soon as it blares on. She leaves it at a level that's just background noise, soft enough that I could almost mistake it for the country music my mother likes to drive to.

We turn out of the parking lot before the bell rings for eighth period. The whole drive to Leila's house there's only the low voices and guitar chords from the radio, the thud-whomp of Leila's car along the otherwise empty road, and the silence of three people very carefully saying nothing at all.

Back at the house, I can feel James and Leila watching me as I walk slowly inside and upstairs, where I turn the corner into the guest room. I shut the door behind me, and they don't try to follow.

I don't hear them come upstairs until a few minutes later, and their feet move past the guest room and straight into Leila's. Her door clicks closed, but soon she's shouting so loudly it doesn't matter. I can hear her through the walls, even with the bathroom between us. I make out a lot of cursing, and I guess she's still talking about what we saw in class. Every so often James's voice interjects, a little lower and more even, and I can't pick out any of his words at all.

I shut my eyes, trying not to let the blank walls around me become another set of screens from which Sylvia Plath's and my mother's faces can flash at me, flipping back and forth. I feel distant again, fogged out, like I'm floating over myself looking down, and I wonder how Leila has the energy to be so angry. Then I think of Mr. Jackson, chuckling as the group presented the creative part of its project. Did he know what they were going to do? And just the thought that he might have is suddenly enough to make me angry too.

———

I must manage to fall asleep or lull myself into a daze, because when there's a knock on the door sometime later, it startles me. I'm sitting on the bed with my back to the wall, and I jump a little, clunking my head.

Three soft taps at the door. A pause, then three more. The door creaks open and Leila's head pokes around it.

"Can I come in?"

I nod.

"James had to go to work," Leila says as she pushes the door the rest of the way open and walks in, closing it behind her. I look at the clock and am surprised to see it's already after five. We left school early, but I've missed the afternoon at Uncle John's office. "But he said he'll come by again on his way home."

Leila stops in the middle of the room, looking around at the cream-colored carpet and walls as if she's forgotten what she came in here to do. She stands there for a minute, leaning back on the heels of her boots, and then sits down in the desk chair. She's turned sideways to face me, but she keeps her eyes on the carpet.

"I wanted to talk to you," she starts.

I want to tell her no. I'm not ready to talk. But I owe her for the way she got me out of English earlier, faking that hall pass from the band director, and I decide it would be unfair for me to stop her. So I shrug and sit there, waiting for whatever she has to say.

"That was awful, what those guys did for their project," Leila says. "I can't believe…" she trails off, shaking her head. She sounds too tired to yell or stomp around anymore.

Then she says, as if she's continuing a conversation we were already having, "It's not that I thought your mother was crazy."

And after a second of confusion I realize James must have told her what I said yesterday, about why I thought the three of us stopped hanging out in sixth grade.

"What happened was that my mother told me I wasn't allowed to be around Aunt Amy anymore, and that it would probably be easier if I found some new friends and stopped spending so much time with you," Leila says.

"She did?"

I wonder if it has anything to do with what she said yesterday, about not putting her life on hold anymore. I open my mouth to say something else—I have no idea what—but Leila, in charge as usual, holds up her hands to stop me from interrupting.

"It was my fault, though," she says. "That my mom decided we weren't allowed to hang out anymore, I mean."

Was this what I overheard my mother and Aunt Cynthia talking about?

My cousin's voice gets softer. "I told my mom about what happened, that day in the car when your mother took us out for a drive and asked us how fast we thought your car could go. You remember, right?"

"I think I do," I whisper. But I'm not sure anymore.

———

In the front seat, my mother turned away from the road to face us. "What do you think?" she asked. Her long hair fluttered in the breeze from the windows, as if an invisible hand were lifting up strands and laying them back down against her shoulders. "How fast?"

Leila and I, playing our New York City game with our dolls across the backseat, looked at each other. I laughed.

We loved it when my mother acted this way, like one of us, wanting to make mischief and break rules.

My mother was still looking at us, waiting for us to answer, and the road whizzed by outside the car's windows without any of us watching it. But my mother managed to keep steering the car through the twists and turns, as if she'd driven it this way before.

"Well, are you ready?" she asked. Her voice was hushed and secretive. "Let's see how fast."

We were heading up a high hill, the old, cranky car grumbling underneath us, and my mother put her foot to the gas pedal, pushing it down as far as it would go. At the same time, she unbuckled her seat belt, then reached over and hit the button to open the sunroof. The sun blazed in, making the car even hotter than it already was. We were the only people on the road for as far as we could see.

"Ready?" my mother asked again, as we got close to the top of the hill. I giggled, not sure what we were supposed to be ready for but eager to find out.

"Ready," we said, Leila chiming in a second behind me.

Then we were at the hill's highest point, and my mother abruptly lifted her foot off the gas and shot up out of her seat. She twisted her body, threw her arms out to either side, and stuck her head out the sunroof. From where we sat in the backseat, we could hear her shout, a *wahoo* that tore out of her and flew all the way up the hill behind us.

The car kept going down.

Leila and I both had our hands to our stomachs, which felt like they might fly out of our bodies if we let go. But my mother sounded thrilled, and we wanted to do whatever she was doing. Our windows were already open, and at the same moment, without planning it out loud, we stuck our heads out to either side and shouted too. We screamed into the wind, our voices searching for hers.

———

"It was so scary, Soph," Leila says, interrupting my memory.

Scary? I'm so confused by the word I barely notice that Leila's called me by my old nickname.

"But it was a game," I say softly. "Like always."

"No, Soph," Leila shakes her head. "You only thought it was a game because she was always doing stuff like that."

Leila's practically whispering now, but she looks up from the carpet and over at me.

"You remember how, when we got to the bottom of the hill, the car kept speeding along?" Leila asks. I nod. This I remember for sure.

"Aunt Amy took her head out of the sunroof and sat down again and managed to stop the car just before we went through a red light. But I was so afraid it would never stop."

216

I feel like someone has glued me here, my legs to the bed and my back to the wall, like I'm part of a sculpture. Or maybe like I'm finally feeling the fear Leila felt that day, the whole time I thought we were playing.

Leila keeps going, telling me more of the story I thought I knew.

"When we got back to your place, we went down to Aunt Amy's studio and she set up an easel and some watercolors for us to play with while she worked. And then she said she was going upstairs to the bathroom and we should behave ourselves while she was gone."

Leila stops, drops her eyes back to the floor.

"I remember," I tell her. Now I'm whispering too. I'm not sure where Leila's story is going, but I don't want to interrupt her until she gets there.

"It seemed like she'd been gone for a while and I really had to pee, so I took the spare key for your apartment from the drawer and told you I was going upstairs. You stayed there painting."

I'm still stuck in place on the bed, and I stare down and press my palms against my thighs. What I really want now is to hold them out toward Leila, telling her to stop. But I know I need to hear the rest.

I remember standing in front of the easel after Leila left the room, swirling blue and yellow and red together with

217

my paintbrush, humming along to my mother's music, not keeping track of how long anyone had been gone.

"When I went into your apartment, I didn't see your mom anywhere," Leila says. "I called out for her and she didn't answer. When I got to the bathroom, the door was closed, and I knocked on it and called out again. She didn't say anything, but I heard a noise from inside, like something falling on the floor."

Leila doesn't have to tell me how scared and nervous and confused she was, standing in the hall outside the bathroom, leaning forward to put one ear against the door. I know because I felt the same way less than two weeks ago, the day I came home from school and hurried through my apartment, calling for my mother, because something about her unfinished painting and unlocked studio seemed off.

My mother didn't answer then either.

"I knew I shouldn't go into the bathroom if someone was in there, but something about it felt strange, so I decided to open the door if I could." Leila's voice is shaking now, and it sounds like she has to force out each word.

"The door was unlocked, and when I looked inside, Aunt Amy was standing in front of the sink. She was holding a glass of water, and there was a prescription bottle open next to her. There were a few pills on the floor, like maybe the bottle was what had fallen down and made the noise I heard.

"She was just swallowing a pill when I opened the door, and she was holding more in her hand—too many for her to just be taking a painkiller. But the door creaked when it opened, and she looked up. She saw me and jumped and dumped out the water and stuck the pill bottle in the cabinet really quickly, before I could see what it was."

My stomach feels like it's trying to climb up my throat and out through my mouth.

My first coherent thought after Leila stops talking and my stomach stops rolling is this: my cousin has actually seen a part of my mother that I never have.

Leila caught my mother in the act of swallowing the pills, but I've only ever seen what comes after that. The white capsules spilled across the night table, the half an inch of water left at the bottom of the glass, the unmoving woman on the bed. Her still hand and dangling feet; the slight breeze of air from her mouth, tickling my face. The voice on the other end of 9-1-1.

Leila takes a deep, raggedy breath, and I look up and meet her eyes.

"I told my mom about the car and about what I saw afterward, with the pills in the bathroom," she whispers. "That's why she said I couldn't be around Aunt Amy. She was afraid I would get hurt somehow."

So she didn't come to the phone when I called, stopped

saving me a seat at lunch, and told James I wouldn't be over anymore after school. On the other side of town, in our tiny apartment, my mother told me only that she needed help remembering to take her medication, and I promised to remind her. She never told me why she wanted help in the first place.

There are so many emotions swirling through my head that if I opened my mouth, I bet all that would come out would be a long, incomprehensible beep, or a burst of static, like a piece of electronic equipment malfunctioning. I can't even name all the things I'm feeling. I just know everything that happened in the last five years is rearranging itself in my brain all at once.

"I had no idea," I finally tell Leila, the same thing James said to me two days ago.

But my voice is angry, not surprised.

Why did no one tell me any of this sometime in the last five years? Why have I, the person who takes care of my mother every day, been the one in the dark? Why did Aunt Cynthia get Leila out, but not me?

Leila interrupts me, speaking much more softly than usual. "I know," she says, in a way that makes me think she really does know how angry and confused I am.

And then she adds something the Leila I used to know, my old best friend, would have said.

"I sort of wish I hadn't told my mom anything," she says, "because it just meant that I left you there to take care of her by yourself, and I didn't even have a chance to explain it to you. That doesn't seem like it was right either. I'm sorry, Sophie."

For a few minutes we sit there quietly, my mother and Aunt Cynthia and the memory of that afternoon with the car and the pills filling the room around us. I breathe in and out, trying to clear my head.

"Me too," I finally tell her, so softly I might only be mouthing the words. "I'm sorry too." Sorry for not speaking up. Sorry for all the things I thought about Leila when, really, I had no idea what was going on in her head.

We're silent some more, until I start to feel like I can move again, like the memories and ghosts squeezing into the room with us have stopped crowding me. Then Leila clears her throat, and I'm afraid there's something worse I haven't heard yet.

"So I think James likes you," is what she actually says.

I stare at her for a minute, and then we both start to laugh. I'm amazed that we can talk about these two things, my mother and James, in the same conversation. That it doesn't have to be one or the other—happy or sad, my mother or my life. Maybe it can be like the axis of the graph, right in the middle, everything at once.

221

When I'm by myself again in the guest room, I stare up at the ceiling, waiting for it to turn into a projector screen again. This time I tell it what I want to watch.

I divide the screen into quadrants, like a scene in a sitcom where everyone on the show is doing something in a different room. In one corner is my mother, painting in her studio. Next to her there's me, shaping ground beef into patties in the kitchen, my homework on the table behind me to finish later. In the third box, under mine, is Leila, standing in front of a music stand and scatting into a microphone, then stopping and starting over from the beginning of the song. And in the last box is Aunt Cynthia in her kitchen, still in her work clothes, starting to chop vegetables for dinner.

If this were a real sitcom, one of us would pick up the phone and call the next person, who would call the third, who would call the fourth, and somehow it would turn back into one picture, all of us in the frame together.

But that doesn't happen on the Cynthia-Amy-Sophie-Leila show. None of us picks up the phone. Instead, we stay in our quadrants alone, repeating our routines, on and on and on.

Cut, I tell the show on my ceiling.

I lie there, listening to Leila sing along to a jazz CD through the wall, and I realize I'm not upset with my cousin anymore. I understand why she told Aunt Cynthia what my mother did in the car that day and about finding my mother in the bathroom swallowing those pills. I understand why Aunt Cynthia told Leila it wasn't safe for her to be around my mother after that, even though the voice in the back of my head is still asking *what about me?*

But I don't want it to be like that anymore. I don't want each of us to be cut off in our own boxes, unable to pick up the phone.

I fling the covers off and go over to the desk, where the stack of books I need to read and homework assignments I have to do gets taller every afternoon. But instead of getting to work, I stare out the window, into the backyard where I buried the veggies from my pizza at my sixth birthday party. I think about everyone who was there that day: Aunt Cynthia and Uncle John, my mother and me, Leila and James and our other classmates and their parents. I think of James yesterday, telling me to let him know if there was anything he could do to help. I think of Natalie, including me in her afternoon with Zach even though we'd just met.

I don't even know how to put what I'm hoping for into words, or even into equations. But I keep those images at the front of my mind—all the people at our birthday party; James offering his help; Natalie and Zach telling us stories at the abandoned house—look out the window, and wish.

TWENTY-TWO

WHEN JAMES RINGS THE BELL ON HIS WAY HOME FROM work, Leila and I both go downstairs. Leila gets there first, and I'm still standing on the fourth step when she unlocks the front door and pulls it open.

James walks in carrying the now-familiar red vinyl pizza case across his left arm and shrugs at our expressions.

"I was hungry, and I figured I probably wasn't the only one," he says.

He sets the case down to take off his jacket, and as I take the last few steps down into the hall, I say, "I was starting to think you had that case surgically attached to your arm."

I make the joke quickly and just as quickly wish I hadn't.

But we all laugh, even though it isn't very funny. And then, just as suddenly, we stop, looking at each other in surprise.

"*That* hasn't happened in a while," Leila says. There's a

sarcastic edge to her voice, but as we look at each other, slow smiles spread over all of our faces.

My smile feels familiar but not. It feels like looking at the painting of Leila and me on her wall; like remembering burying the vegetables at my birthday party. It feels like listening to someone who knows me well tell me a story about myself.

———

We follow Leila back upstairs to her room because she says she has an idea for our English project.

But when James starts to pass around plates with pizza and Leila pulls out her copy of the poetry anthology, it feels too much like last week when I yelled and stormed out.

So when James hands me my food, I say, "I promise I won't throw anything this time," and we all relax a little bit. We sit cross-legged on the floor as if we're back in kindergarten, in a triangle with Leila at the top. We listen to the soft sound of her flipping through the book looking for the right page. I feel drowsy all of a sudden, like all of my energy has evaporated and I could fall asleep right there, sitting up on her floor.

"Here," Leila's voice wakes me up. "I thought maybe we could do this one. It's by someone named Jalaluddin Rumi." She sounds more hesitant than usual, stumbling over the name, and instead of reading aloud herself, she hands the open book to me.

I read the poem she picked slowly to myself, once and then again. Then I clear my throat and read the first few lines out loud:

> This being human is a guest house.
>
> Every morning a new arrival.
>
> A joy, a depression, a meanness,
>
> Some momentary awareness comes
>
> As an unexpected visitor.
>
> Welcome and entertain them all!

My voice gets croaky on the sixth line and I stop, trailing off at the end and ignoring the exclamation point. I stare down at the page for a moment until the text un-blurs. When I look up, James and Leila are watching me, as if I'm now the one at the far point of the triangle. I pass the book along to James, who reads the rest of the poem to himself, murmuring the words.

He looks up when he's done.

"I agree, we should do that one," he says. "Soph?"

I meet Leila's eyes and nod, and in that moment I finally feel like we're on the same wavelength again.

The lines I've just read out loud—*some momentary awareness comes as an unexpected visitor*—echo around my mind, and I think of the parade of unexpected visitors I've had in my life since moving here.

I close my eyes, and an image falls into my head. It feels like the perfect illustration for our poem.

I interrupt James and Leila.

"I know how we should do it," I say. I sound like Leila at her most bossy, but they don't challenge me when I tell them my idea.

As James packs up to leave, Leila turns her music back on and starts softly singing along. And even though I'm nervous about what I'll have to do next, I head off to bed feeling lighter than I did before.

In art the next day, Ms. Triste doesn't ask me where I've been for the last few afternoons. She just nods at me as I set up an easel next to my desk. A few minutes later, she stops by, peers down at my sketchbook, and offers a suggestion for how to change the angle of the drawing when I turn it into a painting. That's another reason she's my favorite teacher: she says her only job is to offer advice when we need it, and as long as we turn in our projects, she doesn't really care when or how we get them done.

I've decided to paint a larger watercolor version of the sketch of my mother, blanketed by the equations in her hospital bed. She's been in that bed for almost two weeks, and I know Dr. Choi plans to discharge her soon.

For the first time in a week, I concentrate on my painting until the bell rings, steadily sweeping colors across the page and checking the shapes I'm forming against my sketched rough draft.

But the end of class bell breaks my concentration, and I remember what I need to do next.

"Hey," I say, stepping toward Natalie's desk and trying to catch her attention. She's looking down at her bag, stuffing things into it, and she doesn't answer.

"Could I talk to you for a minute?"

She still doesn't look up.

I shift, wait, count to ten in my head. Nothing.

"It's kind of important."

Natalie still doesn't meet my eyes, but she lifts her head and steps to the side so I can walk with her. I don't start talking until we've left school and are crossing the parking lot. I don't want anyone else to overhear.

"When I ran out of the pharmacy the other day—" I take a deep breath. Start over. "The pharmacist knew me because I come in there a lot to pick up prescriptions for my mother."

Natalie still hasn't looked at me, but she slows down, so I'm no longer a half step behind her. Her head turns toward me, and I can tell she's waiting for the rest of it. I haven't explained enough.

"She's been in the hospital since the beginning of the year," I tell Natalie, just like I told James. "She OD'd on some of her pills."

Now Natalie does stop, and I turn to face her. I tell her something I haven't told anyone else. "I found her."

I see her hear it, watch her eyes widen and her mouth open.

"I can't even—" she starts. I wonder if she's imagining it, what it would be like to find Claire that way. "I'm so sorry. That must have been awful." She pauses. "That's why you're living with your uncle?"

"Yeah," I say. I look down at the ground and kick a small rock away from Natalie's tire. Then I realize all I did was answer her question, not acknowledge anything else she said. I nudge open that door in my head, just a crack. "It was awful."

"I didn't know how to explain it," I add. "When the pharmacist recognized me. So I just ran out."

We stand together as everyone else hurries past us, eager to end the school day. Then that really hits me: Natalie is still standing here. What I told her didn't send her running. And maybe it won't—maybe, when my mother comes back, I won't have to give up the people I've found while she's been gone.

When Natalie finally does move, it's only to hit the passenger-side door of her car and pull it open.

"Come on," she says and waves me inside.

———

"Will she be okay?" Natalie asks as she drives. "Your mom, I mean? I should have asked that before."

I lean back in my seat, tired from all the confessions. "She should be," I say. "Once they get her back on the right medications."

I don't have the energy to explain how complicated the idea of okay can be when it comes to my mother.

"I'm sorry I complained so much about my mom," Natalie says after a few more minutes. "It feels petty."

"It's okay," I tell her, even though I've thought the same thing a few times. "You're allowed."

She laughs. "Thanks," she says a little sarcastically.

The car rolls to a stop in front of a house, smaller than Uncle John and Aunt Cynthia's, painted a light purple color with black shutters. Natalie is out of the car and headed for the front door when I realize it must be her house.

"Hey," I call after. "Can I borrow some of your paints— the ones you had in your trunk the other day? I'd like to use some for my English project."

Natalie turns back. "There you go, using your trauma to get something from me," she says, and I laugh.

"I moved them to the garage, and there are some other colors in there too. Take whatever you need. I'll be inside." Natalie crosses the lawn, keys jingling in her hand, and I step into the garage.

There are at least ten colors there, and I look over the labels, imagining how much fun it would be use to them all. But in the end I take just four, shades that we can easily mix to make others.

When I tote the cans inside, Natalie is sitting on a stool at the kitchen counter, and Claire is standing across from her, holding an envelope. I'm afraid I've walked into an argument, given how annoyed Natalie and Claire seem to be with each other most of the time. But it looks like they're actually just sorting the mail.

"Thanks," I call out to get Natalie's attention. I gesture to the paint cans. "These will be great."

They both turn around, and Claire smiles at me and says hello. She tells me she heard what a great job I did on Trudy's plans.

"You should think about architecture," she says.

I smile politely and thank her. I'm not ready to think that far in advance. But I like that Claire sees something there.

Natalie hops off her stool and grabs her bag from the floor.

"Let's go," she says.

She leads me through a hallway lined with photographs, most of which I'm guessing Natalie took. Many of them are shots of her family, her parents and sister, and others are of nature, lakes and forest paths and leaves. They're beautiful, but I understand what Natalie meant about not wanting these photos to be in the art show. Watching her walk ahead of me, with her boots and her pin-covered bag, she seems older than these pictures.

She stops at a bathroom, where she flicks on the light and directs me to sit on the toilet lid. She pulls a box of purple hair dye from under the sink, a comb from one of the drawers.

"I bought it anyway," she says. "I was thinking a streak on the right side." She's tilting her head again, considering me through her invisible camera. "What do you say?"

And I think of my mother. How much she'd love to see me with purple in my hair and would probably urge me to go back and do the rest of my head. How it's something she'd suggest in one of her letters to JKP. How I'd look different when she came home, new in this one way, but not in too many others.

TWENTY-THREE

I'M ABOUT TO LEAVE AUNT CYNTHIA'S HOUSE TO SEE
my mother when I hear Leila turn down the music in her
room, and a minute later my cousin is standing in the guest
room doorway, tapping on the wood frame. She knocks
rhythmically, so that she sounds like James playing the drums.

I stop in the middle of the room, in mid-stride toward the
door. Even after our conversation yesterday, I'm surprised
to see Leila here.

"Are you on your way to see your mom?" Leila asks.

I nod. "There's still a little while before the end of
visiting hours."

Leila looks down. "Could I come with you? I want to talk
to her about something." Her voice is soft, unsure, the way
I'd forgotten she could sound until yesterday. She holds up
the hand that isn't already on the doorframe, where she's

still tapping out a rhythm with two fingers, and shakes her keys. "I can drive."

I wonder if she wants to talk to my mother about the things she told me yesterday, about that day in the car and Aunt Cynthia's rule that Leila couldn't spend time around my mother anymore.

But it doesn't matter exactly what Leila wants to tell my mother. It's not my job to be her gatekeeper.

"Okay," I tell her and follow her out to her car.

Once again Leila keeps the music low as she drives. She still hums along and we don't talk at all on the way to the hospital. But the radio doesn't seem like a weapon in a cold war—and maybe it never was. Instead of huddling against the door, I sit up straight and push the seat back.

When we get there, the nurse at the front desk smiles at me and hands over two passes for the eighth floor before I can ask for an extra. I take them and wonder whether the nurses who think I look like my mother can tell I'm related to Leila too. The thought doesn't bother me.

As I lead Leila up to my mother's room, it feels strange to hear another set of footsteps echoing mine through the quiet hospital halls. With each step—my squeaky sneaker, Leila's boot heel, sneaker, boot heel—I have to remind myself that it's her behind me and I don't need to turn around.

We don't discuss it out loud, but when we get upstairs, Leila hangs back in the hallway so I can talk to my mother first. I hesitate in the doorway and look back at Leila the way I always did when we were younger, waiting for a signal that will tell me what to do next. My cousin nods her chin toward my mother's room. *Go on.*

Then she slides to the floor, her back against the wall, to wait for me. She tips her head back and folds her hands together over her skirt, looking more patient than I remember ever seeing her. And I'm surprised to realize I feel better, knowing she'll be right out here the whole time.

I go inside.

———

I head straight for my usual chair at the side of the bed and plop down, legs out, toes pointed up and untied shoelaces dangling, like I'm posing for my own painting.

I'm watching my hands, which are twisting together in my lap as if someone other than me is controlling their movements, when my mother speaks.

"Sophie?" she asks.

And I realize I've been so preoccupied trying to figure out what to say next that I forgot to say hello at all. It isn't particularly funny, but I'm nervous enough that I start to giggle anyway as I say, "Sorry, Mom. Hi. I'm right here."

"What's going on?" she asks. She doesn't sound confused

or anxious the way she has for the past two weeks, but gentle and curious. Curious about me and my knotted hands and nervous laughter, about the new purple streak in my hair.

Curious about me the way Claire probably is about Natalie; the way Uncle John is when he asks about my day.

Curious the way I usually am about my mother, but the way she, for the last two weeks, hasn't been about me.

And so I lift my head and answer.

"The doctor's going to be ready to discharge you soon," I tell her. "He can't know for sure just yet, but it seems like the new dosage on your medication is working, and he says you're doing much better."

Then I stop talking and grip the arms of the chair. I don't even know whether I'm trying to hold myself in place or push my body up from the seat so I can dash out of the room. I just know I'm light-headed, like I might fall out of the chair if I don't hold on. I open my mouth. Close it. Open it again and push the words out.

"But I don't think you should come home just yet."

I force myself to keep looking at my mother even though I want to drop my eyes to her feet, my lap, the floor, the trash can by the door. Anywhere else in the room. I force myself to keep talking.

"It's really hard to be the one responsible for making sure this doesn't happen again," I say. I sweep my arm around at

236

the hospital room to show what *this* is, as if my mother doesn't know.

"You tried to kill yourself, Mom."

I say it flatly. It's just what happened, something we can talk about like any other fact we both know. But as I continue, my voice starts to shake, and I have to swallow and sniff to push back tears.

"I don't want to come home on some other day and find you lying there like that again." I think of eleven-year-old Leila opening the bathroom door and seeing my mother at the sink. She has a pill bottle next to her and a half-empty glass of water in her hand. She dumps a cluster of thick white pills from her other hand into the trash.

"I don't want anyone to find you like that again," I add at a near whisper. "But I can't make sure of that all by myself."

Finally, I give my eyes permission to look down. I trace my toes around a square of floor tile while I wait, the white tip of my sneaker squeaking against the linoleum. I'm thinking about our apartment, with the bedroom we share and the chair in the living room with the stuffing falling out and the kitchen with the brightly painted walls and cluttered counters and my mother's art hanging in every room. Each time I've pictured the apartment lately, it looks smaller and more cramped in my memory. Like it's shrinking with us standing in it, and as the walls close in around us, we have less and less time to decide how we're going to get out.

When I lift my head again, my mother is staring at her blanket, fingers picking at threads that are already unraveling. I wonder if she's been pulling at them when I'm not here, the way I do with the blanket in Aunt Cynthia's guest room. Maybe she tells herself, like the imprisoned princess in a fairy tale, that she can get out of this hospital room as soon as she unravels her blanket down to a single strand of yarn. Does she stay awake at night, picking at it?

For a second I think I know what it's like inside my mother's head. She's confused and woozy and guilty and wanting to make all of it—the moods, the medication, the parenting from her sixteen-year-old daughter—stop. Wanting to get out of this blank white hospital room and back to her colorful studio but terrified of what will happen once she gets there. Unable to remember that she's made it through this before.

"I'm sorry, Sophie," my mother whispers.

I shake my head in a *that's okay* gesture. But she isn't actually looking at me. So I clear my throat and say it out loud, even though it isn't entirely true.

A few minutes pass—with her picking at the blanket and me sliding the tip of my shoe around the squares on the floor—before she raises her head and speaks again.

"So what should we do?" she asks. She doesn't sound upset, the way I half expected she would. She doesn't insist that we'll be fine on our own again after a few days. She genuinely wants to know what I think should happen next.

I fight back a stab of anger at the fact that she's the one asking me to decide. I try to ignore the little voice that still wonders, even though I know better by now, *isn't it supposed to be the other way around?*

"I think we should ask Aunt Cynthia and Uncle John to help," I say, surprised at how decisive I sound. "I've been staying with them since you've been in the hospital, and if it's not a problem for them, maybe we should both stay there for a while once you're out of here. The way we used to."

My mother winces. "I'm not sure how your aunt would feel about that, Sophie." She returns her eyes and hands to the blanket and resumes tugging on a thread. I know what's making her anxious now.

"I know what happened," I say quietly, and my mother's eyes fly back to me.

"Five years ago, on that afternoon you were watching us and we were playing in your studio, you tried to overdose, just like this time. Leila found you in the bathroom while I was downstairs painting. She told me about it yesterday. I know Aunt Cynthia didn't want you to stay with them again after that because she was worried about Leila getting hurt."

I flip my palms up on the arms of the chair, an I'm-out-of-ideas gesture, before I say, "But I don't think there's anything else we can do this time."

And then James's voice pops into my head, telling me I should let him know if he can do anything to help. And Natalie's voice from earlier today, offering me a ride home.

My mother isn't the imprisoned princess in a fairy tale. And neither am I. We haven't run out of options at all. We just have to tell people what we need.

"I think it's okay," I tell her softly. "I think if we tell them we need help, they'll want to help us."

We sit there in silence, each of us waiting for the other to make the final decision. Usually it would be me. But this time I want my mother to agree, to help me make the choice. To understand that I'm not giving up on her, just calling in some backup for as long as we need it.

"Okay," she finally says. "Let's see what Cynthia and John have to say."

"Okay," I whisper back.

I lean over to kiss my mother's cheek. I squeeze her hand once and wait for her to squeeze back in answer, to reach up and touch the purple in my hair. Then I leave the room, smiling a soft thanks at Leila as we switch places in the hall. I look on from the doorway as my cousin walks to the foot of the hospital bed, with what feels like a full minute between each clopping step of her boots on the floor. Before I turn away to take up my waiting spot outside, I see Leila stretch out her arms, palms down, over the blanket. She snatches them back, once, twice. Then, finally, nervously, she lowers her hands to touch my mother's feet.

———

Aunt Cynthia and Uncle John aren't home when we get back from the hospital, so I settle in the living room to wait for them, crossing my legs under me on one of the large puffy chairs. Now that my mother has agreed we should ask them for help, I'm full of an antsy energy, tapping my pencil on my chemistry book and jiggling my feet. After two weeks of keeping mostly to the guest room to avoid everyone in this house, I suddenly can't wait to talk to them.

Leila goes straight upstairs, but I don't hear her usual music come on, and a few minutes later she's back in the living room with a book in her hand. She settles into the chair next to me and props her feet on the ottoman. She opens her book and I look back at mine, rereading a paragraph about isotopes I've tried to get through at least three times already. We don't speak.

I wait for the prickly tension from our morning car rides to settle over us, but it doesn't come. And when Leila turns to me with a quick, sympathetic smile, as if she knows what conversation I'm waiting to have with her parents and how

241

much I'm not looking forward to it, I realize why. My cousin is just trying to keep me company.

Now my eyes travel around Aunt Cynthia and Uncle John's living room, which I've hardly been in since the day I got here, and I try to read the furniture and art and scattered coffee table books the way Uncle John might read the floor plan of a house, looking for clues to its owners' lives. The way Aunt Cynthia probably reads the evidence for her court cases, trying to figure out each defendant's motives.

The room is so neat it could have been lifted out of a catalog from a furniture store, the way all the rooms look in Aunt Cynthia's house. The couch and chairs are the same distance from the fireplace on either side, the dark wooden coffee table perfectly between them, the paintings and photos carefully spaced out along the walls over waist-high bookshelves. The books on the table are full of glossy photos; the charcoal gray and yellow and cream in the carpet match the cushions and upholstery exactly. It's nothing like the apartment I'm used to, where all the colors are bold but don't exactly go together.

But when I look more closely, I start to notice signs that people actually use this room. One of the glossy photo books has slips of paper sticking out from some of the pages, as if someone bookmarked the places they most wanted to go or the pictures they liked best. There's sheet music on a stand in the corner, turned to the middle of a song. The science fiction paperbacks on the shelves have creases down the middle from multiple readings, and a few are held together with rubber bands. On an end table next to the couch is a coaster with a mug still on it, a tea bag tag dangling over the side.

As Leila turns a page next to me, I close my eyes, let the image of the room I just looked at fade away, and open them. This time I see it differently, and so clearly I want to run upstairs for my sketchbook: my mother curled on the couch next to that teacup, paging through one of the books of photos, looking for ideas for paintings. Aunt Cynthia is next to her, a thick document forgotten on her lap while she reads the last pages of a novel. Me sitting cross-legged on the floor with my homework or my sketchbook and pencil. Leila at the music stand in the corner studying a song. Uncle John with his work spread out on the table in the next room, still close enough for a conversation.

The five of us, living here together.

———

Uncle John and Aunt Cynthia almost walk right past us, the smell of takeout wafting behind them from the kitchen, on their way to call us down for dinner. Then they see us and stop short, surprise flashing across their faces at the fact that Leila and I are sitting here, downstairs, together.

I'm expecting Uncle John to make a joke about it—*who are you and what have you done with Sophie and Leila?*—but it's Aunt Cynthia who speaks first.

"We picked up some Chinese food," she says, gesturing back toward the kitchen.

Leila stands up quickly.

"I think Sophie wanted to talk to you guys first," she tells her parents. Then she gives me another sympathetic look and leaves the room before any of us can respond.

I smile ruefully and shake my head at her back. I bet Leila will never stop being like this, taking charge even when nobody asks her to.

I turn back to my aunt and uncle.

"I did want to talk to you," I admit. Nervousness is buzzing through my body again and I shift in the chair, sticking my legs out and then pulling them back under me. "Is it okay if we talk before dinner?"

They both nod, and after a moment, they sit down together on the couch opposite me. They stare at me expectantly, and I wish one of them would pick up a book from the table and look at it instead.

"My mother's doctor says she's almost ready to be discharged," I tell them.

Uncle John leans forward, looking concerned, but it's Aunt Cynthia I'm really watching. My words travel across the room to her and she freezes in her seat. I recognize that response, her temporary paralysis, because it could easily be mine. I have the urge to tell her *breathe*.

"She's doing much better on the new set of medications, and her doctor found a place nearby where she can have regular outpatient therapy. There might even be a center in the city where she can go for free if she's approved for a research study."

Aunt Cynthia shifts slightly across from me, the first signs of a thaw.

"But I don't think I can take care of her by myself," I add, the same thing I admitted to my mother this afternoon. "I can't force her to take her medication every day and watch her every afternoon and make sure she gets to therapy while I'm also going to school and trying to have a job after school." *And getting ready for college the year after next. And having friends.*

I can't keep looking at Aunt Cynthia and Uncle John watching me. I drop my gaze to my book, my eyes catching random words—*neutron, proton, noble gas*—that I know I've learned but that, right now, are just bouncing off the outside of my brain without going in.

As difficult as it was to tell my mother that I couldn't be totally responsible for her anymore, saying it to Aunt Cynthia's stiff face and Uncle John's anxious one is harder still. But I force myself to say it again, less tentatively this time, to make sure they know how serious I am.

"It's too much for me to do all by myself," I repeat, my voice insistent and clear.

But it's not just that I can't do it by myself. It's that, for now at least, I choose not to. I choose to have my own life instead.

"And I don't want to do it anymore," I say. I look at Aunt Cynthia. "It's like what you said, about how we shouldn't put ourselves completely on hold for my mother. I don't want to keep having to choose her over myself."

Then, looking at my lap again, I tell them the rest. How Leila finally told me what she saw when we were eleven. What it was like for me to find my mother barely breathing on her bed that afternoon when I got home from school. It's the first time I've described it out loud to anyone. Even when I was talking to Natalie, I didn't tell her about the way I raced up the stairs and called my mother's name and crunched over the cut-up catalog pages in the hallway as I hurried to the bedroom. The way her feet hung off the bed and her chest barely moved.

My voice isn't distant and flat now; it shakes as I talk. But I don't feel panicked the way I did in class the day after it happened, as the clock ticked and I imagined just what my mother might have been doing at that minute the day before.

My heart isn't racing and I don't see my mother's still body in front of me. This time I know that day is in the past. I'm just remembering it, not reliving it.

When I stop talking, finally, and look at my aunt and uncle again, Uncle John's eyes are wide and Aunt Cynthia's face is practically white. She's holding her hands together so tightly in front of her that parts of them are turning white too.

I wonder for the first time if she's a member of our club, the one Leila and I formed unofficially yesterday in my room. The club of people who've seen my mother with pills in her hand or spilling out of a knocked-over prescription bottle on the table next to her bed.

I can't sit still any longer.

I push myself out of the chair and only just remember to grab my chem book before it falls to the floor. I stand there hunched like a monkey, holding it.

I have to ask.

"I wanted to ask you whether we could stay here, my mother and I, until she's doing well enough to be on her own for longer," I say. "I'm sure you want to talk about it before you decide, so I'll just..." I trail off and take a step toward the doorway. *I'll just scram.*

"Stop!" Aunt Cynthia's voice rings out and I turn around. She looks surprised by her own forcefulness. I register in a corner of my mind that Uncle John has gotten up from the couch and is moving toward the kitchen. He murmurs something about setting the table for dinner.

"We don't need to talk about it," Aunt Cynthia says, her voice softer now. "I mean, of course you can stay here. Both of you."

"Thank you," I manage. My legs start to feel wobbly under me and I fall back into my chair, overloaded with relief, embarrassment, and a strange feeling of defeat all at once. I've finally done it, finally allowed that desperate feeling I had in the hospital elevator, of not wanting my mother to come home, to win.

But it feels like a little bit of a victory for me too.

"You shouldn't thank me," Aunt Cynthia says. "It wasn't right to cut your mother off like that. I didn't trust her to be responsible for Leila anymore, and I needed to find a way to take care of my family and myself. But I know she didn't do what she did intentionally."

I think of how angry I got at my mother that day in the hospital, wishing she would ask me about my day, just once, the way I imagined a normal mom would. Even as the voice in the back of my head reminded me she has never been, and probably never will be, a normal mom.

"And it certainly wasn't fair of me to do that to you," Aunt Cynthia continues. "To leave you to look after her by yourself when you were only eleven. I'm impressed by how well you've handled it. But you're right, you shouldn't have had to do it at all."

She pauses for a moment before she adds, "I'm so sorry, Sophie."

Guilt.

That's part of what's kept us all in our separate boxes on the sitcom screen for the past five years, kept us from picking up the phone. My guilt whenever I catch myself thinking that I want to have my own life. Leila's guilt for telling on my mother; Aunt Cynthia's after she decided to leave me to watch over my mother on my own. My mother's guilt, when she's aware enough to think about it, about the ways we've all had to rearrange our lives around her.

"It's okay," I tell Aunt Cynthia softly. I sound calmer and more grown-up than I feel.

We stand up at the same time and look at each other across the living room. I feel like the wall between us has lost a few more rows of stone and mortar. We're both tall; maybe now if we stand on our tiptoes, we can reach over the top.

Aunt Cynthia and I nod at the same time, a silent agreement that we'll try to do better from now on. I think of a few lines from the poem Leila chose for our English project. *The dark thought, the shame, the malice. Meet them at the door laughing and invite them in.*

Okay, I tell my guilt and embarrassment and defeat and relief. *The door's open. Come in.*

Aunt Cynthia walks to the bottom of the stairs and shouts up to Leila. "You can come down now. It's all clear!"

It's the kind of thing I might have expected Uncle John to say, but not Aunt Cynthia. And my surprise must be obvious on my face because when she turns around Aunt Cynthia actually laughs. It's a sound I haven't heard from her in years, except for the day I stood outside my mother's hospital room and eavesdropped on her visit. Her laugh then was sad and slightly hysterical at the same time, but this one is just a natural laugh, ringing and surprised.

And even though a part of my brain is thinking *this is weird* as I follow Aunt Cynthia and Leila in to dinner, I start laughing too.

TWENTY-FOUR

"JUST PICK A ROOM AND PAINT," I TELL JAMES, TRYING
not to sound impatient. "Use your fingers."

"But what's it supposed to look like?" he whines, drawing
out the words, because he knows it will annoy us. "I don't
know what I should be painting."

I snort audibly. James is lying on his stomach on the floor,
and Leila and I roll our eyes at each other over his head.

"Stop making fun of me," James says, without looking up.
He's still whining.

We're sitting in front of one of the house models from
Uncle John's office, which he gave us as soon as we explained
what we wanted to do. The paint cans from Natalie's garage
are arranged around us, along with other colors that Leila,
Aunt Cynthia, and I picked up from my mother's studio.
While we were there, we brought back some of her

251

paintings to hang up in the guest room and in Uncle John's office, which he decided to turn into a temporary bedroom for me. He insists he doesn't have to bring as much work home now that I'm helping him out.

Through the wall, I can hear my mother's classical music in the guest room, and I picture her there painting, surrounded by her finished work the same way she is in her studio at home. My mother spending her afternoon painting counts as a normal day. Later I'll go in there and sit in the corner, and she'll turn to me every so often and ask my opinion on a color or a section of what she's working on.

"The whole point is that it's not supposed to look like anything in particular," Leila tells James. "You can do whatever you want as long as each room looks different." She doesn't make an effort to keep the exasperation out of her voice as she dips her pinkie into the deep red paint and dots it across the white wall of one of the house's rooms. Dip, dot, dip. A few drops splash onto the trash bag we've put on top of the carpet.

"Exactly," I agree. "Here, just pick some colors and see what happens."

As I reach for the black paint and mix in enough white to get a medium shade of gray, I recite the lines to myself. *Even if they are a crowd of sorrows, who violently sweep your house empty of its furniture, still, treat each guest honorably.* The

252

words *crowd of sorrows* make me think of a flock of dark birds swooping in.

With a few calm, quick swipes, I cover another room in the gray paint. Then I use black and blue to make dark bird-like shapes, really just arrows, on the walls. I take a tiny wooden table from Leila's piled stash of old dollhouse furniture and snap off two of the legs. I glue the now uneven table and those two sorry wooden stick legs onto the floor of my gray room. It looks like a wind has blown through and scattered the pieces.

Next to me, James finally grabs the orange paint, swirling it carefully with yellow on one of the paper plates we're using for palettes. When the orange is a little lighter but there's some yellow still visible, he starts to dab the mixture on the floor of our miniature house. Then he adds more yellow, dots and stripes and tiny suns with slanting rays.

"It seemed like it could use something a little more cheerful," he says, shrugging. He's right. The house looks more balanced now, with a bright strip between Leila's angry red and my sorrowful gray.

And the orange-yellow swirl on the floor seems to wake all of us up. Suddenly, we can't grab the paint fast enough, blending and spattering and using the ridges around the edges of the plates to add waves and textures to the plain colors in some of the rooms, making the purple and green

253

and maroon walls look like oceans at high tide. We scatter Leila's old dollhouse furniture, whole and broken, everywhere. We stick beads and dried pieces of macaroni to the walls like we did on art projects in kindergarten. The whole time we're laughing and wildly waving our arms. James dabs me with paint, red and then blue, and I return the favor. I catch Leila looking at us, a grin on her face, her eyebrows raised at me as if to say *see?*

After a few more frantic minutes of painting and gluing, we all sit back at once and survey our work.

"I think we're done," Leila says. She sounds surprised and maybe a little bit proud.

James and I nod. Every room has been painted, the guest house ready for all of its new arrivals. We've already decided that Leila, with her singer's voice, will read the poem to the class. James and I will explain our project.

James pops the lids back onto the paint cans, gathers the torn pieces of our paper plate palettes into the trash, and stands to go.

He looks at me from the doorway as he says, "I have to get ready for tonight, but I'll see you both later."

As Leila and I finish cleaning up, picking macaroni pieces out of the carpet, I glance at the book next to me on the floor. It's still open to the Rumi poem, and I scan the now familiar words. I'm not sure I agree with the last lines, about

254

welcoming the joy, meanness, and sorrow into our houses-slash-lives because they've arrived for a reason, to teach us something, "a guide from beyond." If that's true, why does my mother have to be part of the lesson? I'd rather think that her illness is a random genetic accident.

But as I look at the house the three of us painted, I still think the first part of the poem is right. The only thing we can really do with these unexpected visitors is open the door and welcome them in.

———

The doorbell rings for the first time when I'm halfway through setting the table. Aunt Cynthia and Uncle John almost never use their dining room, but they insisted I use it tonight, Aunt Cynthia climbing onto a step stool to get the fancier glasses and silverware from the backs of the cabinets.

Now she hurries into the dining room in her usual neat after-work clothes and grabs the bundle of knives and forks out of my hand.

"Go open the door," she says, waving me away. "I'll finish putting these out."

When I open the door, James is standing on the front porch, wearing khakis and a button-down shirt, holding a white casserole dish.

"See, I promised I wouldn't bring pizza," he says before I

have time to tease him about it. "There are some vegetables in that, though."

I stick my tongue out at him and he laughs, not at all offended.

He follows me into the kitchen, where my mother is helping Leila roll out the dough for a piecrust. I stop just inside the doorway, not sure if I need to reintroduce James and my mother. Should I have told my mother that James knows why she was in the hospital? She agreed when Aunt Cynthia and I asked if we could have a dinner to welcome her back. But I'm not sure she realizes that everyone knows where she's back from.

"Mom—" I start.

But before I can remind her who James is, she looks up from the dough and smiles at him, the kind of welcoming, wide, present-in-the-moment smile that makes me want to grin back, I'm so relieved to see it.

"James!" she says, coming around the counter toward us.

"Hi, Ms. Canon," James says. It comes out in something closer to the little kid voice I remember, lifting at the end, like he's pleased she remembers him. They both laugh.

I step aside and she reaches for his arm just as the door-bell rings again. When I leave the room to answer it, she's pulling him toward the counter to pour the filling into the crust.

This time when I pull the door open, I know I'll see Natalie and Zach standing in the pool of light on the porch, leaning against each other. They both smile at me, and Natalie squeezes my shoulder as she comes in, as close as she gets to a hug.

"Thanks for inviting us," Zach says. It sounds oddly formal, but he softens it by actually giving me a hug.

"Come meet everyone," I tell them, leading them into the kitchen. I walk them over to my mother first, introducing Natalie and Zach as my friends.

Soon, everyone's talking to one another, Natalie asking my mother about painting and my mother waving her arms around as she answers; James and Zach chatting as they snack on chips; Leila and Aunt Cynthia carrying dishes into the dining room as Leila asks her mother how long the pie will need to bake. I have to grab a spoon and clink it against a glass to get everyone's attention when it's time to sit down for dinner.

James grabs my arm to hold me back as everyone else moves into the dining room. When I look at him, he stares at the floor and shuffles his feet.

"I have off work tomorrow. So I was wondering if you, um, if you maybe wanted to hang out?"

I feel a smile spread across my face, so wide I'd be embarrassed if James were actually looking at me. It's not just his question, it's everything: having my mother back, having everybody there.

But still, I have to ask. "Are you sure?"

James looks at me, as if to say, *why would I have asked if I weren't sure?*

I tilt my head toward the dining room, where everyone is passing plates and pulling out their chairs. The whole messy group of them. *Do you really want to get involved in this?*

But really, he already is.

"I'm sure," he says. We spend about a minute smiling at each other, until he shuffles his feet again. "So, tomorrow?"

"Okay," I say. "Tomorrow."

———

As soon as we're sitting at the table, passing around the food, the conversation picks up again. Now Leila's telling Natalie about her classes—I hear her say something about our English project. James asks Zach about living in New York City.

"I'm hoping to move there for college in two years," he tells him. "I'd love to go to NYU." Something I didn't know about him.

I know no one would mind if I jumped into the conversation, if I told Natalie and James that Leila and I used to want to live in New York too. That maybe someday we still will. But for the moment all I want to do is lean back in my chair, watch, and listen.

Aunt Cynthia and my mother have their heads bent together, and they're talking to each other quickly, excited about something. Every so often, they erupt into laughter, and I wonder what they're whispering about. Uncle John smiles, looking at them, the kind of *what am I going to do with them* smile I imagine he's been giving them ever since that party years ago when my mother introduced him to Aunt Cynthia.

We look nothing like Trudy's family, all with identical strawberry blond hair and the same pattern of freckles across their noses, matching like the pots lined up in Aunt Cynthia's kitchen. We're a mishmash. More like the array of dishes and spoons and forks that might be in the kitchen of a guest house, where people are always coming and going, accidentally taking some pieces with them to be replaced by others that don't quite fit.

But in a way, we do go together. Uncle John, at the opposite end of the table from me, spotted the ways Aunt Cynthia and I are alike when neither of us could see them. There's Aunt Cynthia and my mother, whose heads of identical brown hair tilt toward each other at the same angle as they talk. Natalie loves photography the way my mother loves painting. Zach and James have the same dream of living in New York City. Leila spends as much time practicing her singing as James does his drumming.

And then there's me, who has a little bit in common with each person lined up around the table.

My family.

I don't want to interrupt to make a toast, and I'm not actually sure how I would say everything I'm thinking right now. But Leila and I catch each other's eyes and smile, and then I look over at my mother and Aunt Cynthia.

We don't need to say anything out loud. But at the same moment, the four of us raise our glasses to each other.

ACKNOWLEDGMENTS

There is a world of people without whom this book would not exist. Thanks to my wonderful agent, Suzie Townsend, who loved this story from the beginning and made it so much better. To Kristin Ostby, who acquired the manuscript for Albert Whitman, and Wendy McClure, who shepherded it through the publication process. And to everyone else at Whitman: thank you.

My first handful of pages would never have become a book without feedback from Micol Ostow and everyone I met in Micol's YA writing class at Mediabistro. G. Jules Reynolds, J. Anderson Coats, Meg Burden, and Hannah Ehrlich, beta readers extraordinaire, made the story stronger with every draft.

My friends are an incredible source of support and encouragement, and their joy at seeing my book published has made the process all the more exciting for me. And, of course, my family: my brother, who always makes me laugh ("How's that novel coming?"), my mom, who showed me what it means to love books, and my dad, who was my first writing teacher. I am lucky to have all of you.

ABOUT THE AUTHOR

Sara Polsky writes fiction, essays and journalism. Her work has appeared in *Christian Science Monitor, Poets & Writers*, and various literary magazines. She writes for the blog *Curbed* as well. She lives in New York City. This is her first novel.